For Chris,
hope you enjoy
All the be
S

Susan Rae Jau

METPACK Nº 30.

CLAWS AND ROBBERS

Susan Rae Glass

AuthorHouse™ UK Ltd.
500 Avebury Boulevard
Central Milton Keynes, MK9 2BE
www.authorhouse.co.uk
Phone: 08001974150

© 2013 Susan Rae Glass. All rights reserved.

No part of this book may be reproduced, stored in a retrieval system, or transmitted by any means without the written permission of the author.

Published by AuthorHouse 4/19/2013

ISBN: 978-1-4817-9226-4 (sc)
ISBN: 978-1-4817-9225-7 (hc)
ISBN: 978-1-4817-9227-1 (e)

Any people depicted in stock imagery provided by Thinkstock are models, and such images are being used for illustrative purposes only. Certain stock imagery © Thinkstock.

This book is printed on acid-free paper.

Because of the dynamic nature of the Internet, any web addresses or links contained in this book may have changed since publication and may no longer be valid.

The views expressed in this work are solely those of the author and do not necessarily reflect the views of the publisher, and the publisher hereby disclaims any responsibility for them.

CHAPTER ONE

Saturday morning, 0100 hours

It had been raining earlier, and the pavements were wet and slick on this cold October night in London. The streets stank as the damp weather heightened the smell of the rubbish that lay on the ground, dumped by passers-by and then crushed under the wheels of minicabs as they waited for drunken customers to take home.

Those customers spilled out into the street in droves. There were two wine bars at this end of the High Street, not to mention several pubs, clubs, and pool halls. Every weekend saw them packed with people. This borough of west London just to the east side of Heathrow Airport was known to have the highest youth population in Europe and also was the most ethnically diverse. Its main High Street boasted more mobile phone stores than any other shopping district in this area of Greater London, along with the most establishments open to the small hours. With the mix of young adults of differing cultures and backgrounds thirsty for cheap drink, running a bar here was a good business if one had a late licence – but sometimes a rough one.

Police patrolled heavily along the main stretch of road which ran through the High Street. Every weekend was punctuated with fights, robberies, and a myriad of other street crimes that stretched police resources to their limit.

This night was unusually quiet for the start of the weekend; the patrons of the bars just wanted to enjoy a few drinks and maybe a dance.

A couple walked from one of the bars. They were drunk; their arms were linked, and they supported each other as they stumbled up the road. They moved away from the main thoroughfare where all the cabs were waiting and headed up one of the back streets which would eventually take them to the underground station and the local residential area.

The young woman giggled as the man whispered in her ear. She flicked her long blonde hair over her shoulder and laughed again as she nearly fell over. The man caught her and kissed her hotly, winding his arms around her slender waist. She pulled away and gazed at him through unfocused eyes, stopping him at the mouth of an alley that ran between the back of the shops and the houses near the High Street.

She touched his face and pressed herself against him, her polished nails grazing his cheek seductively. The man smiled and bent his head to kiss her jaw and neck. She pulled him gently into the alley and urged him to push her against the wall. The man could feel the heat rising in his body even though he was dizzy from the drink.

Through the haze of his intoxication, he heard a noise behind him like the snuffling of a dog. He turned to kick the mutt away.

And opened his mouth to scream.

CHAPTER TWO

Saturday morning, 0200 hours

Lauren took the corner at breakneck speed, the rear of the BMW fishtailing as she turned into the residential street. She gunned the engine of the rapid-response car and sped along the road towards the terraced house halfway along. She sounded the siren again – briefly, given the time of night – and the strobing blue lights bounced back off the brickwork of the houses. Brett gripped the inside handle of the passenger-side door and held his personal radio close to his ear, listening anxiously to the fight unfolding amidst the bleeps of the emergency activation alarm.

Lauren slammed on the brakes, and the car came screeching to a halt outside the house, where an Astra and a van were already stopped. She jumped out the driver's side. Brett followed suit, leaping out of the passenger side and tearing ahead of Lauren.

"Foxtrot one on scene!" Brett shouted into his radio.

The two police officers ran up the path to the house. The front door was wide open, and the sound of frantic shouting could be heard from inside.

In the living room, a skinny male wearing only a pair of baggy grey tracksuit bottoms was fighting with Andrew, the probationer, and Dave, the van driver. Andrew sported a bloody nose where he had been punched. The man was shouting at the top of his voice and was struggling against the two officers as they tried to restrain him. Brett waded into the fray, and eventually the three of them pinned the writhing male to the floor.

By the door which led into the kitchen, Sarah was trying to hold on to a female who was struggling to get to the man. In her hand she waved a kitchen knife and sporadically tried to stab Sarah with it.

"Get the fuck off him, you fucking pigs!" she screeched.

Lauren exchanged a look with Sarah. The smell of alcohol was prevalent in the room, and it was obvious that both the man and the woman were drunk. As the woman swiped at Sarah with her knife again, Lauren took out her asp and flicked it to extend it. She held it ready to strike the woman's knife arm as she approached.

"Put the knife down and get back!" Lauren barked.

"Fuck you, pig!" the woman replied.

The woman lurched forward, raising her arm to stab at Lauren. Lauren pulled her asp arm back, but the woman was so drunk that she caught her foot in her other slipper and crashed to the floor face first. The knife skittered away, and Sarah pounced on her back, cuffs at the ready. Lauren knelt beside them to help hold her down.

The woman screamed and wailed about the bump she now had on her head, yelling that the "bitch officers" had smacked her head to the floor deliberately. She then kicked out behind her, catching Lauren on the thigh with her heel. Lauren gritted her teeth against the pain as Sarah grabbed the woman's legs and held them in place with her body weight. Lauren then bound her legs with Velcro ankle restraints. The woman cursed the officers more, made threats, and then tried to spit at them.

Meanwhile, Brett had managed to restrain the male, and Andrew had him cuffed. The male was trying to reach the woman, but Brett and Andrew kept a firm hand each on his shoulders as he sat on the floor.

Lauren took a deep breath and bent over, wincing at the pain in her left thigh. That was going to bruise later. She looked around the living room of the small house. The woman was shouting and bucking as she lay on the living room floor, swearing at everyone around her.

Sarah retrieved the knife and placed it in a weapons tube so it could be evidenced later.

"Fucking pig bitch!" the woman said over and over as Sarah cautioned her.

The male started to cry as Andrew read him his rights, and huge globs of snot and phlegm erupted from his nose and mouth as he sobbed.

Lauren heard on the radio that the second van unit had turned up, as the two suspects could not travel in the same cage. The female officers waited as their male colleagues struggled to put the man in one van and then came back to assist them.

The woman was still flopping around on the floor like a fish on the river bank, and her trousers had started to roll down, revealing her plump overweight stomach and belly-button piercing, which was caked with filth.

Steve, the second van driver, walked in and took in the scene with a look of utter disgust. Lauren laughed at him.

"Oh Steve, slumming it from the posh end of the ground, are we?" she teased.

"Tell me about it. You show me the best sights of the borough, Lauren," he replied, looking down at the woman and avoiding her latest spitting attack.

Brett and Andrew came back in and scooped the woman up with the help of Steve and carried her out to the back of the second van which stood with the rear doors and the cage door open.

The woman now yelled to the street that she was being groped by the male officers and that their female colleagues were filming the show.

The next-door neighbour stood on her doorstep, four small dirty children around her and a cigarette hanging from her mouth.

"Yer fucking wankers! We pay your wages, cocksuckers!" she snarled.

Lauren rolled her eyes as they helped secure the woman in the van.

She watched as both vans drove off into the night, heading for the main borough police station, and then made her way back to her car, where Brett waited, ignoring the tirade of abuse from the neighbour.

Just another typical start to another typical set of nights on this glorious London borough.

Saturday morning, 0215 hours

What had he done?

The words repeated in Robin's head again and again, becoming a relentless rhythm in his mind, fuelling the fear. He came to a stop at a street corner and leaned against the wall of a shop as he tried to catch his breath. He sucked the air into his strained lungs, and his body doubled over in exhaustion.

He had to keep going, but he was so tired, and the panic made him tremble uncontrollably. He rested back against the wall and looked up at the overcast night sky and tried to bring his breathing under control. He had to go on; there was no other option.

Robin wiped at his damp cheeks with his hand and sighed. They would be looking for him soon, when they realised he had gone.

How had it all gone so horribly wrong?

They had left him at the house when they had gone out. There was nothing new in that; they often left him out of their plans. He was not allowed to leave the house without one of them to accompany him. He was essentially a prisoner, and nothing in his life had changed.

The others had been out partying for hours as usual, and when they had returned they had been extra jubilant. They had brought more drink, and the party had continued. He was not told why; he was not allowed to know what his new masters did, but he could tell. He knew exactly what they had done, and that was before they had started replaying it to each other.

Robin had known then that no matter what, he had to escape.

He had slipped out of the house easily enough; they were all so caught up in the majesty of their own existence that they did not notice him there at all, and he ran – ran as fast as he could for as far as he could, leaving false trails in case they tried to track him. It would be bad if they caught him but far better than to be caught in their company when they were found out.

Robin knew he had to get to his flat, grab some money, and then disappear. This was all his fault, and he shuddered as he thought about how he would be made to pay for what he had done. Maybe if he disappeared, the others would be taken care of and his involvement would not be discovered. He could go back to his flat, go back to work, and no one would be any the wiser.

The sound of a dog barking a few streets away startled him. His entire body jerked with terror, and he sprang back into a run, his feet pounding on the pavement as he ran off into the night.

Saturday morning, 0220 hours

The duty sergeant's voice crackled on the radio as he called up Lauren and asked her if she was free to deal with some of the numerous emergency calls that were still coming out via the central control rooms.

Lauren sighed. She would not be free for a while now; they were driving back to the station and had notes to complete after assisting in the arrest. "Sarge, when I'm done, I'll pop into our control room and see what calls still need doing," she said.

"OK, ta, Lauren," he replied. "Foxtrot two-five. What is your status?" he called to another unit.

Lauren shook her head. "This is what happens when you only have six vehicles out on a Friday night," she grumbled.

"What about our buddy borough? Aren't they supposed to help?" Brett asked.

Lauren shrugged. "Pete and Kellie would have called them up. Even though they're supposed to help us out, it's very rare that they do. Not allowed to leave their ground in case it goes tits up their end. Thing is, while it works, nothing will change."

"But what if something really bad happens?"

Lauren gave a hiss and then laughed. "Don't curse it, probbie."

Kellie, the channel one operator in the control room, announced yet another fight at one of the local bars. It frustrated Lauren to hear call after call coming out and to not be able to do anything about it. She knew this was a mindset shared by most of her teammates. However, all that could be done was one thing at a time. There was no point worrying about it.

Lauren pulled into the main building which was the superstation of the borough. It had been built in the early nineties and was in dire need of modernisation. The custody suite was new – less than a year old and state of the art. It had to be in order to comply with the civil rights of prisoners. It did not matter if in the rest of the building the heating or air conditioning never worked and an engineer had to be called out every time one or the other had to be turned on or off. There had been rumours and announcements for years that a refurbishment for the whole building was in the pipeline or that the police station itself was to be shut down and everyone moved to the posh new industrial estate just off the dual carriageway, but nothing ever came of it.

Lauren, having been in the job for eight years, was cynical every time she heard these announcements. The money was always needed somewhere else as a priority.

She pulled into the yard and saw both vans positioned outside the custody cage. The doors of one van were open, and Lauren could already hear the male shouting. The van was rocking, and as Lauren and Brett got out of their car and walked over, they saw Dave standing in front of the open rear doors. He was holding up his mobile phone and was filming the male.

"Will you calm down, sir!" he called. "I am filming you, and there is no one near you!"

The male was inside the caged area of the van. The cage door was still locked, and the male was throwing himself around inside and screaming.

"Stop beating me up!" he yelled. "Police brutality!"

Lauren watched him, a smile on her face. Then Dave put his phone away as three other male officers arrived. He tapped on the cage door.

"Oi, sir, I need to draw your attention to this sign," he said.

The male glanced at the massive board above the first custody gate.

"This custody and yard have video and audio in operation. Your words and actions are being recorded and can be used as evidence." Dave then pointed to the state-of-the-art CCTV camera which was clearly recording. The male eventually became still and quiet.

"Now, sir," Dave said. "Will you please come with me and we can sort this mess out. I'd prefer to walk you in, not carry you."

The male nodded mutely, and Dave opened the cage. He gently took the male by the arm, and then they walked up to the custody suite.

"I'm sorry, officer," he mumbled and started to cry again. "I'm just very upset at the moment."

Lauren walked over to the second van which held the woman and opened the back doors.

The woman, who was still cuffed and in the leg restraints, rocked forward against the cage and spat at her. Lauren moved quickly out of the way.

"You fucking frigid dyke bitch!" the woman screeched.

Sarah and Steve joined Lauren at the back of the van. Cautiously, avoiding the woman's spittle bombardment, Steve opened the van's cage door. The woman flipped her body so her feet poked out and tried to kick at them again. Steve grabbed her ankles and held her firm. She screamed and fought the male officer and then tried to bite Lauren and Sarah on their legs as they climbed into the van on either side of her and grabbed an arm each.

As she was pulled from the van, the woman went still and made herself a dead weight. Her bottom sank to the ground, and it was a struggle for the three officers to hold her up off the ground and stop her from getting hurt.

"Your fella has walked in, madam. Don't make this more difficult for yourself," Lauren said to her.

The woman opened her mouth and tried to bite Lauren's hand. She was heavy, and as she started to struggle again, it was a chore to carry her up the ramp and into the main custody suite. Together they got her into custody, with Andrew holding open the metal doors. It was slow going, as the woman constantly bucked and fought, her yells echoing into the night.

As they carried her into the main suite, the door banged against the wooden benches where suspects usually sat as they waited to be booked in by one of the two custody sergeants. A small twelve-year-old boy sat on one of these benches with his mum. He looked terrified of the red-faced, aggressive woman being brought in.

"Evening, Sergeant Harris, Sergeant Gill," Steve said, his voice strained with the effort of containing the female.

One of the custody sergeants took one look at the woman and ordered her taken to a cell until she calmed down. Sarah, Lauren, and Steve moved her down the corridor to the cells and put her in one of them, exchanging her cuffs for another Velcro strap. After the woman was searched, she was placed on the floor and left locked in the small room.

The doctor would be called to check her and make sure she was fit for interview, but with the amount she had been drinking, it would most likely be the morning CID who would do that.

As the three officers walked from custody, Steve shook his head in disbelief. "And she was the one who called us in the first place?" he asked.

Sarah nodded. "Call came out that her fella was beating her up. When we got there and saw him laying into her, we nicked him and she started having a go at us," Sarah said.

"Nothing like a bit of self-respect and pride, eh?" Lauren said.

Saturday morning, 0300 hours

Lauren read through her notes and then stood up and took them over to the data stamp reader. Brett followed suit, finishing off his sandwich, and they both took their completed books over to Andrew, who was tapping away at a computer.

"Thanks, guys," he said.

"No worries, mate," Brett said.

Lauren then walked back to the table, packed up her lunch, and picked up her tea. Luckily the notes had not taken her too long, and Brett was very adept at the paperwork side of policing. She had gone over his notes too just to make sure everything had been covered. Still, they had only assisted in the arrest, unlike Andrew and Sarah. As they had taken the call and done the arrest, they would be stuck in the station compiling paperwork for hours yet. First there was the crime report, then the arrest report, one for each suspect, and then there were the notes, and as the call had come out as a domestic violence, they had to do it all again in another separate book and inform everyone from the inspector to the detective sergeant on duty.

Lauren always thought it insane that they had to do so much paperwork. It could take hours to complete, and if there was no CID on duty or they were busy, the arresting officer had to do the interview too. That meant waiting around for solicitors or appropriate adults if the suspect needed one and then typing up the taped interview and the case file for court. There had been civilian typists, who had done that part of the job far quicker than the officers, and for less money too, but their department had been shut down and they had been moved or made redundant. It resulted in every officer who made an arrest spending at least three hours doing the paperwork, and that was just for the straightforward, caught-red-handed-on-CCTV crimes.

Every single promise and initiative to reduce paperwork had resulted in ten times more paperwork, and then a cap on overtime when officers were spending too much time on it. It should have been one system – lots of tick boxes and copy boxes and a permanent staff that did nothing but create case files and typing. However, Lauren and her colleagues knew that would never happen, and as long as the service limped along, it would never change.

Lauren walked into the darkened control room, the cup of steaming tea in her hand.

"Hello, folks!" she greeted them brightly.

A large male police officer turned in his swivel chair to look at her. "Ah! I need a result from you so I can get rid of this call," he said.

She walked over to him, squeezing between the computer terminals behind him and the two chairs beside him. "It's nice to see you too, Pete," she replied and then pulled out her pocketbook. "Which result are you after? We've dealt with a robbery, a theft, an assault, and a collision, not to mention helping out with Andrew's and Sarah's bodies."

Pete looked at his terminal. "The theft."

Lauren looked at her pocketbook. "Crime report by Brett."

Pete punched the information on the keyboard and then rested back in his chair.

The young girl in the chair next to Pete nodded up to the large screen which showed the CCTV angles of the yard. "So what was all that crap about then?"

"That was the domestic that Sarah was dealing with."

Kellie tapped a few keys on her terminal. "But she called police wanting us to come and deal with her partner. Why was she nicked?"

"Assault on police. She pulled a knife on us when we nicked her fella for smacking her one. I guess she just wanted us to wag our fingers and tell him off for her."

The civilian at the main controller's terminal laughed. "Not surprising. Were both of them drunk?"

"Oh, yes, they were."

Brett entered the control room and looked earnestly at Lauren. "That's the man asleep for the night. His girlfriend was calling out to him, and he told her to shut up. Romance never dies!"

"Cheers, Brett." She glanced back to Kellie. "Any more calls we can deal with?"

Kellie shook her head. "Plenty, I'm afraid. It's been one urgent call after another. It's not even a full moon." She tapped more keys. "There is another crap call for Smithson Avenue, just off the High Street," she offered, teasing at her short black hair.

Lauren leaned over Kellie's shoulder and looked at the file as the operator pulled it up. She nodded. "Great! Caller states that she can hear a man screaming down the back alley after he walked up there with a young woman a few minutes earlier." She looked at Brett. "Do you want to go and take a look?"

Brett's blue eyes lit up, eager for all the calls he could get. "Where is it?"

Lauren shrugged. "Smithson Avenue is just round the corner. We can walk there."

Brett nodded. "Fine by me."

Lauren grinned at Pete. "Ah, probationers! Don't you just love their keen attitude?" she said.

"I've printed off the call for you, Lauren. When you come back, pop in the front office and see Liv. She's got the wedding photos with her," Kellie said.

"Will do." Lauren walked over to the printer and picked up the sheet of paper. "The call came in an hour ago. Oh well, with a bit of luck they might have come and gone."

Foul laughter echoed through the room.

Lauren read over the sheet and then made her way from the control room. Brett followed her, doing up his high-visibility jacket.

Near the exit from the control room, there was a large metal cabinet against the wall. Lauren poked her head around the cabinet to say a greeting to the civilian station officer in the striped blue-and-white shirt.

"Hey, Liv, how was Hawaii?"

The station officer looked up from where she sat at the desk and the novel she was reading. "Awesome, Lauren. I highly recommend it. You got a call?"

"Yeah, but I'll pop in and see you later. I want to see those wedding pictures. That was such a good day."

Liv played unconsciously with the new gold band on her ring finger. "My family weren't too rowdy, thank goodness. See you later, hon."

The two police officers walked down the corridor and went out into the yard. Lauren took her small LED flashlight out of her pocket and attached it to the front of her high-visibility jacket.

Brett opened the back gate and held it open for Lauren to walk through first.

"For a probationer, you're such a gentleman!" she teased.

Brett smiled. "You know where we're going; I don't."

They walked away from the police station towards the High Street at a slow pace, heading for the two wine bars at the end.

"What time did the call come in?" Brett asked.

"Oh, about an hour ago. It wasn't an urgent one. It may be nothing, but it's best to be sure." She headed down a residential street just off the High Street. "This is Smithson Avenue. Apparently, it's the alley between some houses here."

Lauren turned her flashlight on, and the street was lit up in front of them.

Brett pulled a face as he smelled the rotten rubbish. "Why would anyone come here?"

"It's a shortcut to the tube station up the road there," she told him, pointing to the railway bridge two hundred yards away.

Brett followed Lauren as she walked up the street. She slowed to a halt at the mouth of the black alley. Her blue eyes scanned the dark houses on either side. Stepping away from the darkness, she pressed the button on her personal radio.

"Foxtrot Oscar, receiving eight-five-five," she said.

"Go ahead, Lauren," crackled Pete's voice in reply.

"Yeah, show time of arrival at scene. Who is the informant, over?"

"Resident at number three, Lauren. Kellie is calling her back now."

"Received. Both houses either side of the alley are in darkness, over."

Pete could be heard sniggering. "Eight-five-five, the answer machine for the informant is on. Are you still going to have a look?"

"Yes, yes, Pete. It all seems quiet so far, over."

"Remember the points for the risk assessment, eight-five-five. You must have your body armour on, beware of all hazards, and don't put yourself at unnecessary risk."

Lauren exchanged a look with Brett and rolled her eyes. "All received, Foxtrot. I'll send in the gobby probbie."

Brett pulled a face at her and then looked at the opening of the alley. Lauren stood beside him, and they began to walk slowly along the pavement, the LED light casting strange and sinister shadows. Brett pulled out his torch and turned it on, flashing it over the wet brick walls and the dirty ground. He pulled another face at the litter, which had stuck to the ground and had begun to smell in the damp air.

Lauren's heart began to beat faster in her ribcage, making her Met vest feel too tight. The fingers of her left hand rested on her utility belt, ready to pull her asp or her gas, and her right hand was gently around her radio, ready to call up if she needed to.

She glanced at Brett and was glad to see he had more or less mirrored her actions. He towered above her at six feet and had quite a stocky build. This was his first set of nights on team, and so far he was doing well. He had been posted with her for his first five weeks after completing his street duties course, having only just come out of Hendon Training School. He was older than she was and had worked in a morgue before life in the Metropolitan Police had tempted him.

Lauren stared forward, her light shining the way before her. She frowned, getting the feeling that something was not right.

Brett took a sniff of the air and grunted in disgust. "Lauren, that's not rubbish," he said, coughing.

Then the smell hit her. It was foul in a sweet, decaying, intensely metallic way that was not at all like rotting food. She stopped and looked around at the brickwork of the alley walls. She had been to enough sudden death calls in her time to know that scent.

Brett raised his torch higher and let the light scan the high walls on either side of them, and he gagged.

Lauren was shaking uncontrollably as she pressed the button on her radio. "Foxtrot Oscar one, receiving on this channel, over," she called, trying not to throw up.

"Go ahead, eight-five-five," replied a female voice.

"Guv, we're dealing with a call on Smithson Avenue. I think that you, the skipper CID, and SOCO need to get down here. It looks as though we have a sudden death."

"Received. On my way."

"Foxtrot Oscar five, Foxtrot Oscar," Pete called on the main channel.

Lauren let her eyes follow the scene in front of her. Patterns of blood were sprayed and splattered up both of the alley walls and spread on the ground. Her reluctant eyes traced what looked like pieces of raw meat with sections of white, glistening bone protruding. The wet flesh glinted in the light of her torch, and she found it hard to swallow without throwing up. She looked along the ropes of dark red and purple intestines which lay scrambled on the rain-soaked ground, and she saw the barely recognisable torso of a man wearing the rags of a designer shirt. She felt the acid in her stomach burn and really had to fight the urge to lose her dinner. A head sat on the ground nearby, baby blue eyes staring out of a partially crushed skull with a ripped-out throat.

Lauren took a step back and held her breath. It was not the blood so much as the smell of the ripped bowels and the empty, soulless look of the eyes – absolutely no expression, just a void. She looked at Brett and saw he had turned green.

"I thought you would be used to this," she remarked, exhaling slowly.

"By the time they got to me in my previous job, they had been cleaned up somewhat," he said. "Are we sure it's just one person?"

Lauren covered her mouth.

CHAPTER THREE

Saturday morning, 0515 hours

It had rained during the night, and a soft sheen covered the grounds of the mansion as morning approached. Birds chirped loudly in the treetops of the expansive woodland surrounding the estate, the sounds of the other animals echoing in the air. A predawn mist rolled down the grassy decline to the treeline, and a fresh, woody scent hung in the air.

Marcus took a deep breath and let his violet eyes wander over the darkened landscape. The sky was a deep navy blue, and the almost-full moon hung low in the night sky, waiting to be chased away by the approaching day. He leaned in the doorway of the back patio and sipped his morning coffee. This had to be his favourite time of the day, when the sounds and the smells of the world were waking up.

It was a sheer pleasure for him, one he was extremely territorial over. The calmness of this simple morning ritual would soon be overwhelmed by the commitments of the coming day; such was the burden of running one's own business. There was always so much to do, so much to take care of, that he sometimes wished he could clone himself. He smiled at that thought; now that would be problematic.

Dace, his grey Inuit Husky, padded up behind him and sniffed his hand.

Marcus scratched the dog behind his ears and tapped the top of his massive head. Dace stepped out onto the patio, turned back to Marcus, and barked expectantly.

"Not this morning, Dace," Marcus said in his deep, rich voice. "You go for a run by yourself."

Dace's green eyes seemed to meet Marcus's for a moment; then the dog turned and ran out across the expansive lawn and disappeared into the wood.

Marcus's smile grew wider as he smelled the scent of fresh bread and heard the bakery van pull up. The old stables had been converted into several craft shops and a butterfly house, which had a small cafe bar attached. The bread was for them.

Just another thing he liked about this time of the morning – the pleasantly overwhelming scent of freshly baked bread coupled with his Jamaica Blue coffee and a tinge of diesel as a background.

The van idled on the gravel drive beside the old stables to his right, and the smell of the bread became more pronounced as the driver got out and opened up the rear of the van. On cue, the slamming of the rear door started the cacophony of barking from the sheltered kennels to the left of the property.

The driver waved a greeting to Marcus as he hefted the three trays and carried them into the rear of the cafe. Marcus returned the gesture and then made his way to the sealed-off kennel area to his left.

It started with the kennels, but the entire left wing of the grounds was given over to the animals and the private zoo. The section nearest the house was the dog behaviour centre that Victoria ran.

As he approached, the barking continued and then faded away. He looked inside the wire fence and saw the pack of dogs running around on the grass area, chasing a ball thrown by Victoria.

She stood by the main gate, watching the pack tear off, some yelping with excitement. Her face was flushed, and her blue eyes were bright. Her cropped grey hair was currently dyed pink, clashing with her dark purple tracksuit. She looked at Marcus and smiled widely and then unlocked the gate and joined him.

"Morning bread is here, I take it," she said.

He nodded. "Morning, Mother." He nodded to the pack. "How are they doing?"

"Good. The Rottweiler and the German Shepherd are ready for adoption;

the Staffy is still having issues. I do wish people would not have a Staff without knowing what the breed needs."

"Same old story. Dog equals fashion accessory. In about three years we'll be overrun with Pomeranians and Chihuahuas people can't handle," he pointed out.

Victoria punched him playfully on the arm and locked the gate. "Are you not running with Dace this morning?" she asked.

Marcus shook his head. "As much as I would love to, I have a lot to do today."

Victoria scowled at him. "Ooh, he will not like that, Marcus. That dog can hold a grudge."

Marcus grinned. "Thank goodness I have a mother who can teach me how to be the boss of my dog then. Dace will learn his place."

Victoria laughed and then frowned as she looked past her son to the rear doors of the mansion. Marcus followed her gaze and saw a petite blonde in a black suit standing in the doorway. He could tell by the look on her face that something was wrong.

Marcus approached her and looked down at her delicate features. "What is it, Ingrid?"

Her harsh North Yorkshire accent seemed to be even harder than usual. "Sorry to bother you, boss, but we have received information about a problem which is about to explode, big time."

Saturday morning, 1132 hours

Lauren staggered rather than walked into the hall of the town house which was her home. Well, it was her parents' home, but they travelled abroad a lot, and she paid all the bills on it.

She felt like a zombie, so tired that she wondered how on earth she had got home safe. She could not even remember the twenty-five-minute drive from the station; it was all a haze of sleep deprivation.

Getting off on time after a night shift usually never happened; there was always the last-minute call, the arrest of a shoplifter from one of the three twenty-four-hour supermarkets in the borough. If a unit was free, they had to deal with it.

However, this morning was quite different. After the initial call, the inspector, along with CID, had turned up at the alley, by which time Lauren and Brett had cordoned off the scene and another few units had come to assist. It had taken all but two cars off the road, leaving them to tackle the calls that were still coming out. A neighbouring borough had helped out as much as possible, but they had their own division to police. The command team of the borough had created extra teams to work on busy Friday and Saturday nights, but they had finished an hour before the body had been discovered. As a result, all of Lauren's team had had to stay on to be debriefed and had not been released until after ten in the morning.

Lauren sighed and rubbed her sore eyes, feeling the frustrated tears burn. Sleep – she needed some sleep before going in and starting the dance again. She took off her coat and dumped it in the hallway, not wanting to waste the effort to hang it up. She staggered up the three flights of stairs and almost fell into her bedroom.

The bed had been made, and by the bedside table on her side was a folded piece of paper. She sat down and picked it up, unfolding it and reading it. Lauren shook her head, screwed the paper up into a ball, and threw it in the bin. Relationships! There was a very good reason why she hated them and did not have them.

"I had to go home and get ready for late turn. You could have at least bothered to call me and let me know you would be late off."

Whatever! She could read the snide sarcasm in the words and wondered again if this man was the right one for her. He had an arrogant personality, which she usually hated, but for some reason she really liked him. Part of her wanted to go and get her phone and call him and tell him to get lost with his stupid little note, but she was just too damn tired.

Perhaps she would have a word with him about leaving little notes like that the next time she saw him. They were both in the job, and he knew the score. She did not make a fuss when he was off late and they had made arrangements. It came with the territory.

Lauren stripped off and hid under her covers, making sure that her earplugs were in to drown out the main part of everyday life in London. Most of the citizens of this fair city were blissfully unaware of what went on after dark. She closed her eyes and shuddered, recalling the bloody mess she had found: the arm ripped from the torso, the ball of the shoulder joint glistening in the moonlit alley. So much blood and flesh, the sound of rats scurrying and leaving the body as more units screamed to a halt around them.

Her pulse thundered loudly in her ears, and she could feel the panic rising within her. She knew the image would not go away any time soon. She opened her eyes and stared into the darkened room.

A pair of dead eyes stared at her from a bloody, severed head.

Lauren screamed and sat up but found that she was alone. She was sweating and shaking. She lay back down again, trying to calm herself with slow, even breaths, and eventually she began to drift off.

Saturday afternoon, 1435 hours

Detective Sergeant Jack Ladd stood near the mouth of the alley, scowling at the local residents with his grey eyes. They all stood out on the front steps of their houses, craning their necks to look up the closed-off walkway. No one could see much; the SOCO had put a tent up over the crime scene, and officers tempted by overtime at short notice covered both ends of the alley.

He looked at the area around him and shook his head. It was a dump; there was no other way to say it. There was litter and dirt everywhere, which left an underlying smell even when there wasn't a dead body. Every few minutes the shadow and deafening rumble of a plane coming in low to land at the airport sounded overhead.

He looked at his inspector as he spoke with the duty officer nearby, making sure he could hear every word. As one of the sergeants of Murder Squad Team 4, this would be his investigation to lead. His governor was just doing the introductions.

Jack saw a small, thin lad stick two fingers up at him from where he stood in front of one of the houses. Charming, he thought and curled his lip at the little horror. The kid ducked back into the house, telling his mother how the nasty policeman had pulled a face at him. Great – another complaint. With his close-cropped hair and rather hard features, he did appear quite intimidating.

"Where are the officers who found the body?" DI Sprite asked.

"Their team are nights at the moment. The whole team were here until eleven this morning, when they were all debriefed and sent home," replied the late turn duty officer.

"What time does night duty come in at?" asked Jack.

"Nine o'clock. The officers have been told you will want to speak with them."

DI Sprite nodded and turned his gaze to Jack. "Have you been to have a look yet, Jack?"

"I sneaked a little peek, guv. I didn't think SOCO would let me in. From what I could see it was a real mess."

The DI nodded. "Well, they have only just been able to find out that it's only one body."

Jack glanced back over his shoulder to the alley and frowned again. "Have we got an ID yet, guv?"

"I've got a unit going to the address we found on the licence in his wallet," said the duty officer. He then shook his head. "I don't know how we'll even begin to make an ID. I've also got some PCSOs going through the CCTV for last night."

Jack looked impressed. "CCTV covers that area, does it?"

The duty officer pointed along the street. "This was a robbery hotspot. Local council put it in all the back streets from the High Street. We have a good rapport with the operators, and they contact us if anything happens. The alley isn't covered, just the entrance."

All three men turned as a small figure clothed in a white suit came out of the alley. Two men carrying a zipped and sealed body bag on a trolley followed the petite black woman. She looked at the three of them, and the expression of horror in her eyes was obvious.

DI Sprite walked over to her. "Well, any idea?"

"At this moment, I can't tell you a lot," she said in a thick Glasgow accent. "All I know at this time is that he was ripped apart. I don't know by whom or what."

"Definitely ripped apart?" Jack queried.

"Aye," she looked up at him. "Again, I can't tell you how yet, or if it was a human or an animal."

"So what have you been doing in there for the last ten hours then?" he asked.

She raised an eyebrow. "Attempting to identify and gather up all the body parts," she said as though he should have known. She nodded behind her as three more SOCOs came out of the alley carrying small boxes, each covered with a body bag. "He's been spread about quite a bit."

Jack appreciated the dark humour she was attempting. It compensated for the horror of having to use the crime-scene equivalent of a shovel to scoop up the victim.

She walked off with her colleagues to the coroner's van.

Jack looked from her to the alley and made a face of disgust.

"I want you to check the hospitals and see if any of their mental patients have done a runner," the DI told him.

Jack gave him a blank stare. "You think a madman did this, guv?" he said in disbelief.

The DI met his gaze. "Of course. What else could it be?" Jack stared down the alley and caught a brief glimpse of blood on the wall. He heard his boss laugh slightly. "Don't go all spooky on me, Jack. It was some crazy mental person on drugs with a weapon we haven't found yet."

Jack sighed and smirked. "I know. I've just never seen anyone who could do that. Someone who had that kind of strength." He was lost in thought for a moment and then shook himself back to his senses. "I'll get Ted and Andrea to check out the hospitals."

"Well, there are three hospitals which have mental health wings on this borough alone," the DI told him.

"Bollocks!"

Jack watched his inspector walk away, a grin on his superior's face. He matched Jack's height but was about twice as wide. He had played rugby for the Met when he was younger and had been the head of Murder Squad Team 4 for three years.

Jack had always wanted to join the murder squad and had pushed through his probation to get it. He now studied the alley in front of him with the two PCSOs standing at the mouth and wondered if that had been a good idea after all. There was something about this case that already did not feel right.

He would have to stick around and speak to the officers who had found the body when they paraded that night. They might have some idea or clue as to how one man could have ripped another to shreds.

He looked to the house where the kid had gestured at him and found a rather dirty young woman glaring at him. As he walked past her to follow his inspector back to the police station, the girl gestured to him with more vehemence than her son had done.

Jack was glad to see she was excelling in her role as mother, the first teacher.

CHAPTER FOUR

Saturday afternoon, 1600 hours

Marcus frowned and pinched the bridge of his nose. He stood in his office situated on the ground floor of the left wing of the mansion. His telephone was pressed to his ear, and he winced as he fielded yet another panicked call from one of the branch alphas.

"Yes, Jacques, we are looking into it," he repeated the phrase again, but the man on the other end of the line did not seem to take heed. He sighed. "Jacques, listen to me. I will sort this out – or do you doubt me?"

The man hesitated for an instant too long for Marcus's liking before he relented and the conversation finished. Marcus hung up the phone and turned to look at the massive wide-screen television hung on the walnut-panelled wall.

He had turned the volume down when the phone calls started coming in, but he could still hear the reporter relate the events of the "horrific and brutal murder" in this "quiet and unassuming" area of West London. The initial report described the murder as so violent that it appeared a wild animal had attacked the unfortunate man. It had been this revelation that had sparked the influx of calls from branch alphas around the world demanding that he tell them what was going on and, if it was a pack problem, what was he doing to solve it.

Marcus sighed and padded over to one of the sofas by the window where Dace lay and scratched the ears of the animal. Dace wagged his tail slightly and rolled onto his back, making Marcus smile with affection.

He took in all the activity behind the reporter: the PCSOs standing guard on the crime scene, the search officers in their dark blue overalls getting ready to comb the streets for clues, and the numerous marked police vehicles parked everywhere.

The scene then flashed to pre-broadcast footage of the borough chief superintendent and the usual announcement that the murder squad were now involved and were doing all that was necessary to solve this crime as quickly as possible. Then a helpline number rolled along the bottom of the screen with an appeal for information.

Marcus shook his head, the anger rising in him again, and he pushed down the urge to throw the remote control at the screen, knowing that in his state of mind it would probably punch through the wall and into Victoria's office next door. He should have known about this much earlier; how could this crime have happened under his nose without him knowing about it? In this respect, the other alphas were correct to question his authority. This situation had arisen in his back garden, and he had been completely ignorant of it. It was too late to do anything about it now, as the locals were involved and there was exposure.

Exposure. It was not a good word at all, and one he did not want associated with him. He needed to find out what was going on and deal with the problem before any of the others thought to challenge him. This was now his problem and exposure could finish them all.

Marcus sat on the sofa next to Dace and stared up at the ceiling, trying to get his thoughts in order. He wondered how this situation could be made to go away. Paying off corrupt officers was not an option, and even if he could have managed it, the press were a law unto themselves. It might not be as bad as they thought; it could have been just a frenzied attack or even a wild dog; according to Victoria, there were certainly enough wild strays being sent her way lately.

The door to his office opened, and Victoria walked in briskly. At her heels came her personal assistant. This one was tall, young, and very handsome, with ebony skin and a muscled physique. Marcus observed the young male dogging his mother's steps and wondered if he was also the latest of Victoria's lovers. They were few and far between, and she had only begun to indulge in this vice after his father had died thirty years ago. Marcus did not begrudge her; she deserved her pleasures and her happiness.

Victoria held her computer tablet in her hand. "Most of the pack has responded to the message on the network site. So far, most of them are accounted for. None in this area seem to be missing, and none appear to be hiding from us." A look of relief pulled at her eyes. "This seems to be a normal murder."

Marcus wanted to share the feeling of relief, but something held him back. He was uncertain, and that was a good thing to be. "I've sent Ingrid and James to have a look around. Just to be sure."

Victoria nodded. "Have you told the others yet?"

Marcus's jaw tightened. "Unfortunately, they have been contacting me, and they want answers."

Murder left a thick atmosphere wherever it struck. The street was filled with police vehicles; some were vans, and some were minibuses with teams of officers piling out and preparing to search the surrounding area. The alley and the street were still cordoned off to allow the fingertip search to take place with minimal interruption, and news cameras from various channels observed the circus from behind the blue and white plastic tape.

Ingrid posed in front of one such camera, her back to the scene. James held the camera and filmed all that was going on. The data was being streamed directly back to Marcus, where he could go over the footage and look for any clues. The news that so far no members were missing was a great relief, but to err on the side of caution, this had to be looked into.

"You take the street. I'll take the alley," Ingrid ordered.

James nodded, hefted the camera onto his powerful left shoulder, and pretended to be going live.

Ingrid raised the microphone and started to give a speech to the camera. While her voice sounded, she let her nose seek out better information. She concentrated on the alley, flinched at the still very pungent smell of blood and faeces, and then sought what was under it. There was chicken, kebab, and vegetables, all rotting and old. Her mind assessed and dismissed older and more decayed scents immediately, and then there was the hot scent of an aroused male. She frowned and identified the salty smell as the murder victim, the scent carrying to the blood. A female scent almost made her sick. The smell didn't indicate that the woman had been aroused, thank goodness – that really would have repulsed her – but it was something else. The woman was not in good shape; she did not smell like a healthy human should smell, but that was the fast-food generation with all the processed crap oozing out of their pores.

Ingrid probed the scent of the female further; it was the most unusual. Then there was another scent similar to the first. She gasped and met James's yellow eyes, and she knew he was detecting the same scents she was.

"I've got four," he said too quietly for any normal hearing to pick up.

"Wank!" Ingrid cursed. She pulled out her phone and pressed a speed dial button. It was answered immediately. "Boss, this is a right bloody mess. We've got six of the bastards, and none of them are pack."

Marcus finished the call and placed the phone back on his desk very gently, and Victoria could feel the deliberate restraint coming from him. She stared at her son, and he could hear her heart thundering in her chest.

Everything was about to change.

"I want to know how this happened," Marcus said quietly. "We must start our own investigation. These rogues did not just appear; someone in the pack must have made them."

Victoria turned to Stefan and nodded. He turned and left the room, and she looked back at her son. There was so much advice she needed to give, wanted to give, but she could not interfere. This was his burden, not hers.

"Could this be a rival? The timing of this incident cannot be a coincidence," Victoria suggested.

Marcus gave her a look. "I do not have any rival, Mother, and as for timing, I have told you I am not looking yet."

Victoria rested her palms on the table and looked down at him. "Marcus, you cannot delay for much longer. You need to start looking for a mate, or a rival will take the pack from you. You know this, and you have played bachelor for too long."

"Mother, enough!" He sighed. "When this is done, I will start looking for an alpha, but not before then. This is far too important. Again, we cannot risk exposure."

Victoria sighed and then turned to leave. She glanced back at her son as he picked up the phone and began making calls. If she had not known better, she would have believed he had created this crisis deliberately in order to delay the search for a mate. Well, if there was a rival out there, they would have the misfortune of having to go through her first.

Saturday afternoon, 1645 hours

Jack walked into the main CID office of the police station and looked at the team of detectives milling around and answering calls. The DI was upstairs with the borough senior management team and their on-call senior officer discussing what the next moves would be. The street and the alley were both closed off still, and the search teams were going along every inch of the surrounding area looking for any evidence.

Initially it looked as though a wild animal had attacked and killed the victim, so the tactical support group had been deployed to the borough as well as a firearms unit. The collators were trawling through the intelligence reports and coming up with a list of venues for any potential rendezvous places for any incidents. The CCTV showed the man entering the alley with a blonde female but did not show her exiting, which did not make any sense.

PCSOs were still conducting house-to-house enquiries, which would be gone over again once the rest of the team arrived. For now, the local detectives and the two from his team who were on call were making all the necessary phone calls.

As Jack headed for one of the desks that had been cleared for him, a tall brunette in jeans and a T-shirt walked over to him.

"Hey, skip," Andrea greeted him in a thick Welsh accent. "I just got off the phone with the local hospitals. All of their mental health patients are accounted for."

Jack sighed. "What about the victim? Any leads on him at all?"

She nodded. "His name is Jake McDonald. A family liaison officer is with the mother now. Apparently the victim is well known to us. A five-year check reveals that he was a drug dealer on the borough."

"Was he still dealing?"

"Not for about two years. From what we can gather, he was beat up pretty badly by a rival and just gave up the life. He even found a job."

Jack's mind began to make connections. "What about the old associates?

This could be another attack. Maybe he wanted to get back in the business and make some money."

"The intelligence unit are compiling a file of known associates and business rivals. They will also get a list of current dealers in and around his old patch. The TSG will have some fun knocking on a few doors tonight." She gave an evil grin.

So at least there were avenues of enquiry to follow. He would be staying on until night duty started and would speak to the two officers who had found the body. He had already gone through their notes and their statements, but he always preferred a face-to-face chat. Sometimes there were hunches and guesses that could not go in notes but that could help. It would also be a great way to introduce himself to the team.

"What else do we need to do?" Jack asked.

A male officer with greying hair walked up. "We should look into the animal side of it as well, skip," he said. "I've done some digging and found that there's a private zoo that has a dog sanctuary on the grounds."

"What the hell is a dog sanctuary?" Jack asked, pulling a face.

Ted looked over his pocketbook notes. "It's run by a company called Moonscape Incorporated. The woman who runs it is an animal psychologist. She takes stray and dangerous dogs and makes them viable for adoption."

Ted moved to the computer he had been using and punched a few buttons. He brought up the internet page. Jack's eyes widened at the sight of the woman with the bright pink hair surrounded by numerous dogs of different breeds.

"Oh, Vicky Harper!" said a gruff voice behind him. "Her show is fantastic!"

Jack turned to look incredulously at his DI. "You know her?"

"Course. She trains dogs. Her son runs Moonscape Inc., the fifth most successful business in the world." The DI paused and then frowned. "She's not a suspect, is she?"

"Fifth most successful business in the world. Boss, how do you know that?"

"The missus watches a lot of telly," replied the DI a little too quickly.

"I was just looking at the potential animal attack angle, boss," Ted said. "They have a private zoo and a dog sanctuary. I just wanted to cover all the bases."

DI Sprite looked at Ted. "What about the other leads? Have we got the list for TSG yet?"

"Intel unit is still working on it, boss," Andrea said.

"Well, we'll speak to Moonscape as well, but I want the dealers in this borough checked as a priority. The chief super told me about a murder that happened a year ago where a junkie was hacked to bits with a machete because he couldn't pay his bill. Happened not too far from out scene, and with the vic being a former drug dealer, this could be a turf war thing. I've spoken to Gizzy Gilbert from the gang task force to give him a heads up if this is a drugs murder."

"Right, boss," Ted said and then walked off.

Andrea followed suit.

DI Sprite looked at Jack. "Any news from the coroner yet?"

"No, boss. Maybe it's an animal attack done by a dealer. You know, like fighting dogs and such," Jack suggested. He picked up the evidence bags that contained the initial digital photographs from the scene. Even after looking at them constantly for hours, he was still disgusted by the sheer viciousness of the attack. "I mean, is it possible that a dog could do this to a person if ordered to? It looks unreal – he doesn't look human anymore, just looks like leftovers."

The DI nodded at the computer screen. "Once we eliminate any involvement with Moonscape, maybe we can ask Ms Harper about that. If anyone knows about dog behaviour, she does. Did you know she has a van going around London picking up strays? Free of charge – doesn't bill anyone."

"So when I go to speak to her, I take it you will be joining me," Jack said.

"No, because I have a million and one bloody actions to supervise, plus the press to suck up to." He grinned. "Besides, why would I have a dog and bark myself?"

Jack rolled his eyes. "You had to go there, didn't you, you twit."

"Respect your supervisor, Jack. I still sign your yearly report."

"You did what!" Victoria exclaimed.

Marcus looked up at his mother from where he sat behind his desk in his office. "The officers investigating the murder want to come and speak with you. I arranged the appointment for here tomorrow."

She was tempted to slam her hands on the desk but knew in her anger she might shatter the wood. "You know how I feel about the police, Marcus. How could you?"

Marcus did not flinch at the look of betrayal in her eyes. "That was years ago, mother. Things have changed in the police. Besides, refusal would look suspicious."

Victoria took some deep breaths. "You should have asked me first. I do not like being made to do this."

"I will be there with you, Mother," he assured her. "Primarily, they need to come and check out the zoo and the dog sanctuary. Make sure there were no escapes."

"I will kill them all before I allow them to take my pack away from me!"

Marcus stood up and walked around the desk. The anxiety was rolling off her in waves. The smell of panic made his nose itch. He placed his hands on her shoulders and felt her mood ease slightly.

"We will open our doors to them. Show them we do not have anything to hide. Which, in relation to this murder, we do not. This was not a pack killing, so we can meet the police, and we will be eliminated from their enquiries immediately."

Listening to his voice, Victoria knew he was right. They had to be as upfront with the police as possible. She shuddered at the thought of meeting with them. Her last encounter with the authorities had not gone well, and the very idea of having to sit in the same room with police terrified her to her core. It was an old fear, from a lifetime ago, but still able to cripple her all these years later.

Marcus squeezed her shoulders gently. His violet eyes met hers, and there was a fierceness in them that looked effortless and very much like his father's. "I promise you, Mother, not just as your son but as your pack leader, that I will be there with you and nothing bad will happen to you."

The promise calmed her instantly, pushing her old fears away to the dark corners. She needed to Change; she wanted to run and could feel the urge twitch her muscles.

Marcus nodded to her, and she left the office, trembling.

Ingrid was waiting outside. As Victoria left, she walked into the office with a tablet in her hand. "Boss, I've compiled a list of pack members that work in the mainstream," she said.

Marcus frowned. "Are all pack members accounted for?"

"Not quite. There are a few we still need to contact, some of them on this list. These members work with humans. They are placed in close contact with humans and are not supervised by the company. There is a possibility that one or more of them could have made the rogue pack."

Marcus frowned. "Bit of a reach, isn't it?"

Ingrid shrugged. "Best to cover all the bases. I've called them up and ordered them in for interviews with you from tomorrow." She delved into her pocket and pulled out a small plastic bag with a paper in it. She handed it over to Marcus. "This was recovered near the scene and carries the scent of the rogues. I figured that if anyone made this pack, you could use this to sniff them out."

Marcus laughed at her genius. "Ingrid, what would I do without you?"

"A challenge to the pack is a personal challenge to me. I'm your head of security; I cannot allow this tosser to take the piss."

CHAPTER FIVE

Saturday night, 2045 hours

"Police operator. What is your emergency?"

"Er, there seems to be a wolf in my back garden."

"A wolf, sir? Is it your wolf?"

"Of course not. I have a cat, not a dog. My cat is scared."

"What is the dog doing?"

"It's a bloody great big wolf, and it's digging up my carrots. My cat is too scared to go out."

"If there is a stray dog in your garden, you need to call the RSPCA."

"It's not a dog, it's a bloody wolf. It's massive and yellow coloured."

"Have you tried chasing the dog out of your garden, sir?"

"No, I fucking haven't! You need to get someone out here. It could be like that murder that happened in the town centre!"

"Sir, if you continue to swear, I'll have to terminate the call. You need to call the RSPCA and get them to come out or go outside and bang a pot with a wooden spoon to scare off the dog."

"I told you, it's not a bloody dog … Oh shit, it's looking at me!"

Saturday night, 2100 hours

Inspector Kent stood at the front of the parade room and faced her exhausted team. This was only the second night shift of seven, and already most of them had had enough. Behind her on the wall were six photographs of young teenagers, each mug shot trying to look tougher and pout more fiercely than the last.

Off to one side, Jack sat in a typical Met Police uncomfortable plastic chair that was falling apart and studied the team. He had called the office number for Vicky Harper's dog training school and had been put through to her son. He had been more than happy to set up an appointment to speak with her at Lunar Park estate, her home address, for the next day. Despite what he had said, the DI was going to try to join him, no doubt with a copy of Ms Harper's latest book for her to sign. Jack had spent some of his time researching Vicky Harper; it seemed that dog training had come a long way from basic commands to sit delivered in a firm voice.

The inspector glanced over her shoulder at the photos on the board. "These are the regular prolific robbers that we need to be on the lookout for tonight. I'm sure you are familiar with them all. They frequent the residential area around Beachwood Park. Crime squad would be very grateful if you could pick them up, as they are all named suspects in several robberies in the borough."

The listening officers scribbled notes in their respective pocketbooks as the daily briefing continued. They went through burglary figures, high-risk missing persons to be on the lookout for, and recent lost or stolen vehicles. Finally, Inspector Kent glanced towards Jack.

"This is DC Jack Ladd from the murder squad. He's here to give us an update on the murder."

She nodded towards him, and Jack stood up and took centre stage. "Firstly, I would like to thank you lot for the great job you did last night preserving the scene and all. It did not come in as an urgent call, but the quick thinking of the responding officers and the team have been noted. Initially, we believe this to be a rival drug dealer killing, but we are keeping all other lines of enquiry open. I would like to speak to the officers who found the body – even though we have your statements, I need to speak to you further."

"So what about the animal attack the press has been going on about?" Pete asked.

Jack grinned. "We're thinking a vicious dog. Maybe one trained by a rival dealer. The victim was in the drugs trade up until two years ago. It is possible that he may have tried to get back into it. At this stage we are still gathering all the information we can. The press will be sniffing around, so I don't need to tell you to watch what you say. We are speaking to them through the press office and your super at the minute, and that's how we want to keep it."

"Any suspects yet, Sarge?" Andrew asked.

"Not yet. We have released the CCTV footage of the blonde female seen with the victim going into the alley, but so far, no results. House to house came up with very little information. Unfortunately the locals are so used to the noise from the bars kicking out that they've turned a deaf ear to anything which may have been useful. At the minute we have TSG, and on the briefing there is a list of RVP locations in case we get any further incidents."

"Will there be any?" the custody sergeant asked.

"The murder seems very personal. I would like to say no, but with these kinds of incidents we always get the usual people coming into the front office with information."

Liv groaned and put her head in her hands. "Station office is shut tonight!" she said to laughter.

"Also, there has been a stop and search authorised on any known drug dealers in the borough. If this is a drug thing, we want them brought in, especially if they have any weapons or dogs that are known to be out of control and have been known to use both to police their turf."

The custody sergeant waved his hand. "I'm closing custody tonight!" he said to more laughter.

"If this is not a one-off thing," Jack said, "I do not want anyone taking any chances out there tonight. Call it in, get backup. Late turn have been authorised to stay on until two in the morning. The crime scene is still open, and the alert state for the borough has been raised. Don't be a twat and try to be a hero."

Jack finished up his part of the briefing, and the duty sergeant then announced the postings for that night. Once he was done, the officers filed out of the parade room to begin the handover from late turn to night duty.

Lauren and Brett remained behind, and once the room was empty, Jack walked over to them. Lauren stood up and gave Jack a hug.

"Hey, coyote!" Jack said. "I couldn't believe it when I saw your name at the bottom of all this mess."

"The Met obviously don't want to solve this if they've given it to you," she retorted. "We still on for Sunday dinner next week?"

"Yeah, the missus can't wait to show you the new kitchen now the bastard is finally done."

Lauren looked at Brett, who was frowning at them. "We were at training school together," she explained. "So how are Sandra and Vinnie? That boy keeping you on your toes?"

"Course he is. He takes after me, Lauren. Right, let's get a brew and chat about what happened last night, you little shit magnet."

Saturday night, 2120 hours

Jack Sullivan never really stood a chance. His mother had never wanted him but had found out she was pregnant too late to get rid of him. She never cared for him, never tried to raise him, and never showed any interest in what he was doing. He had got in with his current gang when he started secondary school and had played truant more times than he had attended. Social services were having meetings about this, half of which he could not be bothered showing up for. Big deal. To them he was just another broken child from a broken home with an alcoholic mother and a stepfather who spent his mum's child allowance on yet more booze, fags, whatever.

Jack stood with his friends near the bus stop on Beachwood Road. He was having a cigarette and watching the twats at the bus stop. The idiots had probably been working all day for sod all. The good thing about the social is that he had got a brand new telly and games console out of them, because he had said it was not fair that he did not have one and that he was being bullied at school over it and that if he had one, he could go back. Suckers. You could get anything from the social for free; all you had to do was bleat about how bad your life was and how that new music system might just cheer you up.

Jack laughed to himself and observed the dozy cow waiting for the bus. She was chatting on her mobile phone, possibly to her boyfriend, as she was very flirty. Her handbag was hooked loosely on the fingers of her free hand, and she was swinging it back and forth in a very tantalising way. She was not paying any attention to what was around her and was letting everyone who could hear know what she would be doing when she got home.

Easy pickings. The woman should just hand him the bag and be done.

He looked at his mates and signalled to the woman. The five others moved carefully to the bus stop and surrounded her, and still she was unaware of what was happening.

Jack would never in all his days forget the look of sheer astonishment on her stupid face as he ran up to her, grabbed the bag from her hand, and ran off up the road. His friends followed, and they made their way down a back street and over the fence into the park.

They all ran through the park until they got to their usual meet point so far in that at night that they would not be seen from the outside. Right down the back near the motorway was an overgrown area of bushes where they could huddle, smoke, and check the contents of the bag.

Jack laughed as he arrived at their spot and waited for the rest of his friends. Calum grabbed the bag and searched the contents. He turned his nose up, and the bag was thrown into the bushes.

"What the fuck you doing?" Jack asked. "There could be money in that!"

"It's shit," Calum said. "We should have gone for the phone."

"What, and have it blocked?" Jack sucked his teeth and moved into the bushes. "Seriously, blood, you are so vexing me right now."

Jack got down on his hands and knees and began to search on all fours for the scattered belongings from the bag. He heard a noise behind him and, thinking it was the police, moved further into the undergrowth. He turned to see what the noise was but could not see a lot in the darkness which pressed in around him.

He could hear his friends calling out to him, asking him where he was. Then he heard it: a series of low, menacing growls.

Saturday night, 2140 hours

Lauren, Jack and Brett stood in the night duty kitchen that was situated in the custody suite of the police station. Lauren had just completed the required checks on the car she would be driving that night as all drivers were required to do when taking over a vehicle at the start of each shift.

As she was an area car driver, she was waiting for a call to come out, but the control room had been advised that the murder squad needed to speak to them. Once the checks were done and the logbook signed, the trio moved into custody to get a drink each out of the team tea locker.

"So this scene, is there anything about it you can tell me that isn't in your notes?" Jack asked.

"It made me want to throw up," Lauren replied. "I've never seen anything like it, Jack."

Brett was sipping his coffee. Jack looked at him.

"Well?" he prompted.

"I used to work in the morgue before I joined the job."

Jack grinned. "So no post mortem visit for you then? Lucky I'd had breakfast before I went on mine." Lauren laughed as she remembered his reaction and Jack continued. "I chucked up so much that I thought I was going to lose my stomach."

"You get used to it," Brett said, shrugging. "But this was different. I'd never seen them at the scene before."

"So why do I get the feeling that you're holding something back? Out with it."

Brett sighed. "When I got over the initial shock of the body, I remembered seeing something very similar before. Do you remember the lion mauling on the news a year ago?" Jack and Lauren shook their heads. "Well, anyway, this handler got caught in an enclosure with a pride of lions during feeding time. That's the worst time to go anywhere near them. They mauled him, and he was killed. We got the body, or what was left of it, and I have to say the similarities are incredible."

"You believe it was a wild animal, not a man?" Jack asked.

Brett shrugged. "I'm not trying to step on any toes here, Sarge, but I've seen a lot of dead bodies killed in all manner of ways. From what I've seen, no man with a weapon did that. The victim was ripped apart by something with very sharp teeth and claws."

"Mad dog?"

"Dogs? It would need to be a pack of them to cause the amount of damage we saw."

Jack cursed.

The radios crackled, and then Pete's voice came out over the channel. "Stand by all units. Foxtrot one, any available units, immediate response required. We have a robbery five minutes ago on Beachwood Road."

Lauren looked at Jack. "I need to take this," she said.

Jack gave her a smile. "Mind if I join you?"

"Can you still run?" she asked.

She tossed the paper cup in the bin and ran out of the kitchen. She pressed a button on her radio. "Show Foxtrot one, Foxtrot Oscar."

"Sending it to your terminal, L. Can I have a unit to back up Foxtrot one? There are six reported robbers involved."

"Sounds like Sullivan and co.," Brett said to Lauren as they ran out of custody.

Jack followed them out of the building and jumped into the back of the BMW as Lauren gunned the engine. She turned on the two-tone sirens and lights as a couple more units accepted the call and eased her way out of the packed yard. Pressing the horn as she turned out of the station, she accelerated down the road.

This was the part of response team that Jack missed – the adrenalin rush of an urgent call, being in the area car as it sped along the streets and being flung around corners at insane velocity. It was exhilarating speeding over a small bridge and feeling his stomach in his mouth.

They made it to the main dual carriageway and slowed down as they hit traffic. The cars in front slammed on their breaks, causing Lauren to bring her speed right down to a crawl, and then some of them got out of her way. One car remained in front of them. Lauren sounded the horn, but still the car would not move. She took in the traffic around her to see if she could slow down even more and undertake the car in front.

Brett, gripping the door handle, shook his head. "Are they even looking in their rear-view mirror?" he moaned.

Jack wound down his window and stuck his head out. "Oi! Get out of the way, you idiot!"

Lauren touched the sirens and sounded the horn again. The driver in front seemed to come awake. They panicked and swerved into the other lane, almost hitting another car.

"You stupid muppet!" Jack yelled as they shot past.

Lauren grinned and squeezed the accelerator once more.

Within minutes they were at the scene. The van unit and a late turn unit were already there, and one of the officers was speaking to the victim.

As Lauren, Brett, and Jack got out of the car, Kenny Robbins walked over to her.

"Hey, Lauren. It looks as though it's Sullivan and his little gang." He glanced over his shoulder at the victim. "She made a positive ID when shown some images."

"Do we need to do a drive round?" Lauren asked.

Kenny shook his head and nodded over towards the darkened park. "They ran in there. TSG are on the way to help, and the dog unit are en route. We're just waiting for the guy from the council to come and open the gates."

Lauren walked over to the gates that stood ten feet tall. She grabbed the iron railings and pulled herself up to see if she could get in, wedging her foot halfway up. She could see nothing in the darkness.

Kenny grinned up at her. "Nice view," he said, looking up at her rear.

She smiled back. "Nice aim!" she replied, glancing at her foot, which was level with her face.

Saturday night, 2145 hours

Robin watched anxiously out of his hotel room window as the officers put the male in the van. He did not know who the male was – possibly one of the numerous illegal immigrants in the area. At first he had thought the police had arrived for him and had hastily packed his bags, ready to flee again, but they had only come for the male, who was apparently wanted for begging offences.

Robin breathed a sigh of relief and looked back at the television on the cheap sideboard. The news was rife with the murder from the night before, and Robin had watched nothing else since booking into this hotel.

He had given a false name and paid in cash, and the receptionist had not asked him for identification. The bored-looking male was probably glad he actually had some money up front. This hotel, situated near to the motorway and within a convenient distance of the airport, had been a four star hotel. That was until the local council had decided to use it to house immigrants awaiting hearings and homeless people seeking emergency accommodation. It had been nice, once, but now the smell of human detritus hung heavy on the air, and every corridor was filled with these poor, desperate souls. The hotel stank of body odour, booze, and drugs. This was why Robin had chosen it.

The assault of so many scents threatened to make him sick every time he inhaled, even when he remained in his room, but it masked him from the others who would be looking for him.

He wondered if they had been watching the news and were on the run too. They were still very clumsy; the murder was evidence of that and would make them easier to find. He just had to keep his head down, and maybe, just maybe, everything would be fine.

Robin walked over to the sideboard and poured another shot of rum into the plastic cup and, with a shaking hand, raised it to his lips. He had taken a chance going out to supermarket, but he needed food and he needed the drink. He had made sure he went during the busiest part of the day, again in an attempt to mask his scent, and had run in and out as quickly as he could. He gulped the rum down and sat on the lumpy double bed and studied the news footage of the murder scene and listened to the reporter going on and on about the ferocity of the crime.

Suddenly, the door to his hotel room buckled and shattered, splinters spraying across the room. Robin screamed and dove behind his bed for cover. Wood dust hung on the air, and James walked into the room. Robin cried out again as he saw him and rolled up into a ball, rocking back and forth.

James moved around the bed and stood in front of Robin, his yellow eyes glaring.

Ingrid marched into the room, her nose wrinkling in disgust at the stink. She looked at the sideboard and picked up the bottle of rum and then walked slowly over to where Robin crouched. He looked up at her and whimpered.

"Robin, if you are intending to run, you should abandon all personal habits," she said and then tutted. "When I could not track you, I tracked your favourite tipple, you idiot."

Ingrid bent over and lifted Robin up with one powerful arm. Robin struggled but did not have the will to resist. She threw him out of the hotel room, and he crashed into the wall of the corridor. She stepped out after him and hauled him to his feet.

"Take care of the damage, James," Ingrid instructed. Then, holding Robin firmly, she walked him from the hotel.

Saturday night, 2200 hours

"Six-five-eight to Foxtrot Oscar, receiving, over," Kenny said into his personal radio.

"Go ahead," said Kellie's voice in reply.

"The dog unit is about to go into the park. TSG will follow them in, and we will wait for them to call us for any arrests," he said.

"Received."

Kenny watched as ten TSG officers stood at the entrance of the park. The gates had now been flung open, and the dog unit was getting ready to go in. The two German Shepherds were keen to get started. They sat patiently on the ground, waiting for the order from their handlers, and had their ears pricked up with eagerness.

Sergeant Tom Haliday stood talking with one of the handlers, letting them know the general layout of the park. Lauren watched the scene and felt a twinge of restless jealousy as the dog handlers finally disappeared into the park, followed at a short distance by TSG.

Kenny looked down at Lauren. "I know. I want to get some of the fun as well," he said.

She met his eyes and let some of her anger show. "I think you get enough of that," she said quietly.

He let out a small laugh. "You can never have too much fun, Lauren."

"What? Like leaving little sarcastic notes? Sarcasm can be fun," Lauren snapped.

Kenny hung his head. "I'm sorry. It's just – you didn't call me to let me know where you were. Jackie didn't call me either, and it just hit a sore spot because of what she did. I'm sorry …"

Lauren shrugged. "I'm not Jackie, and don't you dare compare us. Leave another note like that, and we're done."

Lauren walked away from him and joined Brett and Sergeant Haliday. The sergeant's dark brown eyes were fixed on the main gate, watching and waiting for any kind of movement, prepared for the robbers to come running their way.

"Sarge, I heard Jack Sullivan was amongst the robbers," Brett said.

The sergeant looked at him. "He was identified by the victim. Why?"

"He's on my tasking list. I would really like to nick him if possible."

Sergeant Haliday nodded. "I'll see what I can do, Brett."

Jack was tense. The lights were still throbbing in the darkness, pulsing against the tops of the trees on the other side of the fence. After the drive, he stood out of the way, letting Lauren and her colleagues get on with their jobs. He wished he had had the time to pick up a radio on the way out so that he could hear what was going on, but the other officers were in the same position. There was a tension in the air. Everyone there was ready to run into the park at a moment's notice.

The radios began to crackle.

"Ninety-two receiving, Oscar zero," came the voice of one of the dog handlers.

Sergeant Haliday pressed his PR button. "Go ahead."

Claws and Robbers

"Sarge, we're at the rear of the park, and the dogs aren't getting anything. Looks like they've done a—" The voice broke off, and the radio went dead.

Brett sucked his breath in sharply and touched the volume button on his radio, straining to hear. The dogs in the park could be heard barking frantically.

"Oscar unit, receiving, over!" called the sergeant.

The dogs stopped barking abruptly. Then shouting could be heard in the distance. It was TSG.

"Stop right there! Down on the ground, now!"

Jack got off the car and stepped forward anxiously. Sergeant Haliday ran towards the park, ordering two officers to stay at the gateway.

"Yeah, Ninety-two, from Oscar Zero. We have one youth detained. Repeat, one youth detained."

"On my way!" panted the sergeant.

Lauren followed at his heels, running into the darkness. She could see the numerous torchlights ahead of her and used that as a guide. Brett overtook her, along with Kenny, but she pushed herself and managed to keep up.

They reached the dog unit and TSG and slowed to a stop. Jack caught up with her and stood there panting for what felt like hours. He grimaced and grabbed the stitch in his side, cursing himself for not running more often.

He saw one of the dog handlers straining to hold on to his dog as it stretched to the very end of its lead on hind legs, bellowing at a small lad. The boy looked very young and gave the impression that he was a rabbit caught in the headlights of an oncoming vehicle.

The TSG team stood nearby. The handler called off his dog, and it obeyed. The lad seemed to calm down once the dog was removed. He was visibly shaking and looked at all the officers who around him with wide, petrified eyes.

"Please, get me out of here!" he pleaded.

Lauren stepped towards him, moving through the members of the TSG unit. "You're Jack Sullivan, aren't you?" she asked.

He nodded at her, although through his trembling it was hard to spot. "Please, help me!" he said again.

A TSG officer gave a harsh laugh. "Why should we help you?" he asked.

The young lad jumped as the huge man spoke to him, glaring down at him. He then looked at the dogs, which were both being restrained by their handlers, and felt faint.

Kenny stepped forward and caught the boy before he fell. "Hey, what is it?"

Jack looked up at Kenny. "We were attacked by the dogs," he said, nodding to them.

"Impossible!" shouted one of the handlers. "They've both been on the lead the whole time."

"I told him I would introduce him to PC Asp if he didn't come out of his hiding place," the TSG officer said.

Lauren shrugged – nothing wrong with that.

"No!" Sullivan said. "I could hear the dogs. They attacked the others," he pointed towards the bushes. "They're still in there."

Sergeant Haliday looked at the dog handler, who shrugged. "I don't know, Sarge; we only found one robber."

"So you and your little chums were attacked by dogs, eh?" asked the TSG officer. "Did you get the breed? Would it have been a Pomeranian?"

Jack Sullivan looked blank for a moment. "Er ... Yeah, it was."

Jack stifled a laugh.

Kenny passed the lad to Brett. "Do the honours then," he said.

Brett began to caution him and then led him away from the scene.

Jack shook his head and turned to follow the officers back to the car. His foot trod in something soft. "Shit!" he cursed.

The TSG officer following him with the flashlight went to laugh and then stopped abruptly. "I don't think so, Sarge."

Jack frowned and looked at the officer, who, even in the darkness, he could see had turned green. He got his own flashlight and shone it down onto the grass.

His stomach jumped, and he just about held onto the canteen curry he had enjoyed earlier that evening. "What the hell?"

His voice trailed away as he saw what looked like a pile of mangled meat. He followed the trail of blood past the TSG officer and shone it into the darkness behind him. His jaw dropped as he saw the flesh and blood dripping from the branches of the bushes.

"I want this place sealed off, now!"

CHAPTER SIX

Sunday morning, 0600 hours

Victoria ran through the woods, her thoughts chasing her down like animals after their prey. She could feel the muscles of her legs bunch and stretch with each length and again revelled in the utter freedom she felt.

All this was hers – her territory and her land. It belonged to her family, her boy, who was not such a boy anymore, but he was hers too. He had grown up so fast in her mind, and she had no idea where the years had gone. It seemed like only yesterday that he had first opened his violet eyes to the world and she had fallen in love with the pink, squirming baby.

She was tense and angry and really needed the run this morning. The threat to everything she held dear was such a tangible thing that it felt like a shackle chaining her down. Her instincts were in overdrive. She had Stefan look into the political positions of the other alphas behind her son's back. Marcus would be angry with her when he discovered her spying, but she had always been the better statesman than he. She did not trust the others, especially the European alpha, and something deep inside told her that they would use this murder as an excuse to challenge Marcus.

Natural instinct, Stewart had called it. Animals and humans alike shared the power of instinct, but only the latter ignored theirs on a regular basis. She would cry at the memory of her husband as she thought of him, but not until she Changed. This moment was about the run, the exercise, the getting rid of all the negativity and frustration with a simple activity.

Stewart had been the love of her life; over six feet tall and muscular, with blonde hair and blue eyes which became violet, he had been an elegant, gentle man who had adored Vicky just for being Vicky. He had taught her the power of the run, the way it allowed her to leave all her problems behind and then return and face them stronger and harder than ever before.

Marcus was their only child; he took his height and hair colour from her father, but his eyes and his physicality were all Stewart. She had no regrets about her life with him or the choices she had made, even though in the beginning they had been made when she was in a terrible state of mind. Stewart had been a lover of life, a traveller, and an entrepreneur. Marcus did have fun, but he was a thinker, would read the classics, and his nature was quieter and subtler. He knew everything that went on in the pack.

Well, everything apart from who had created the rogues that now threatened to expose them all. There were extremely strict rules and regulations about recruitment into the pack. Personal and professional criteria had to be met and trials had to be endured at the mansion before the Bite was bestowed. That was the best description: bestowed. It was an honour to become pack and not something to be doled out like the free toys in a child's fast-food box. All the rogues had to go; they had broken the law, committed a murder, and had got the police involved. No member of the pack would ever or had ever killed a human either by accident or design, and any rogue that did was executed or worse. It was unnatural for a wolf to hunt a human; that only happened in the darkest winter in the most extreme of circumstances, and part of being pack meant access to the legitimate network of hunting grounds around the world.

That access was something the pack had enjoyed for years without fear of exposure and without making any mistakes. There was such a vast network of support that Victoria found it astonishing that a pack member had gone against this philosophy and, in doing so, had risked the lives of everyone under her son's care.

Now that they had the culprit in custody, the damage to the pack could be limited. She had been shocked when Ingrid and James had returned to the mansion, the female head of security dragging a bloodied and beaten Robin behind her. She had obviously indulged in a little punishment on the journey back, and Victoria could not blame her. She herself had tried to gain access to the prisoner, but Marcus had given her an order to stay away, and she had had no choice but to obey.

Victoria skirted the trees with ease, loping at a steady pace. She picked up the scent of Dace and made a sound for him to join her. She stood and waited for him, and he bounded over to her like a pup greeting the den mother. He nipped at her snout, and she nipped at his neck to let him know that they would run, not eat, and he fell in behind her. She glanced at the beautiful animal and then turned and ran back to the house at full pelt. Dace yipped and followed.

The smell of coffee and toast grew stronger as Victoria neared the mansion, along with the unmistakable scent of a fried breakfast. Her stomach growled, and the noise sounded in her throat as she drew closer.

Marcus had prepared everything for her today. He was making a special effort to boost her morale, knowing she would have to face the police later. He knew how much she loathed government authorities and was trying to appease her for making the appointment with the police behind her back.

He would lead the interview; that was his job. He wanted to direct it and find out what the police knew in his unassuming way. Victoria had dreaded this day. Had the exposure of the pack become inevitable with the modern media world and social networking? They had taken precautions against a Change being caught on CCTV, but camera phones were something else entirely.

Marcus had set up private health clubs and gyms twenty years ago to be used by the pack and run by the pack. He had wanted an exclusive and safe place for the pack to Change, or just be themselves without fear of discovery.

Now it seemed they would be revealed to the world anyway. Robin had gone behind Marcus's back and created his own rogue pack for reasons she could only speculate about. It could be that a rival from one of the other branches was responsible and was controlling him. Marcus had been prime alpha for thirty years now, and still there was no alpha female by his side. It was wrong, and he knew it, but her son was too picky when it came to love. Now it was very possible that this would be his downfall.

Sunday morning, 1000 hours

Jack walked into the CID office with a mug of tea in hand. Ted and Andrea were already there with the DI, sorting out the photographs in the small section of the office which had been given over to them as the incident room. The rest of his team had been brought in due to the events of the previous night and were busy on phones and tapping away at computers.

DI Sprite looked at the graphic digital photographs as they were pinned up on the white board; he then turned to Jack and took a bite out of his bacon roll. "Kind of puts you off eating a bit, eh, Jack?"

Jack concentrated very hard on sipping his tea and not on the tomato sauce dripping from the bacon roll. "The photos don't do it justice, sir."

"Whoever did this thought they were doing a bit of justice," the DI said. "Crime Squad have just lost five of their most prolific robbers."

Jack raised his eyebrows. "SOCO actually managed to identify five bodies amongst that mess?" he asked incredulously.

Ted turned to look at him. "Do you want to hear the best news, Sarge?"

Jack did not, knowing it would be bad, but nodded anyway.

Ted went to one of the desks provided for them and picked up a blue clip folder. "These are the names of all the drug dealers and associates that may have had a problem with our first victim."

Jack took the folder and browsed through it. He met Ted's dark eyes. "All of them accounted for? No forensics or anything to tie them to this?"

"Yep, and whilst the incident in the park was going on, officers were talking to each of the potential suspects and making sure their movements were verified. Most of them are on tag, so that was easy."

"Damn!" Jack said and then looked at the DI. "Well, what now, guv?"

"All the officers who were present last night have been questioned?" asked DI Sprite.

Jack nodded. "I didn't get home till gone three this morning, and I turned up at the scene a few minutes after the robbery. I can account for their movements."

"And no one saw anything?"

"No, guv, nothing at all. Not one of us went into that park until it was opened."

Jack frowned. In the space of mere minutes, five more-or-less healthy youths had been ripped apart just like the man in the alley. No one had heard anything or seen anyone else in the park.

He yawned and drank down the rest of his tea. "Have we arranged a press conference? Appeals to the public?"

The DI nodded. "Me and the chief super are doing one in an hour. Have you seen the paper this morning though?"

Jack shook his head, and the DI tossed him a copy of the Sunday rag. The headline read, "Clawed Vigilante Stalks Town Centre!"

As Jack read the article, which was full of the best creative writing he had seen in a while, Ted finished pinning the papers on the board. It showed a map of the division with red pins marking the places where each murder had occurred. They were quite close together, separated by a built-up residential area and the main road leading to the motorway junction.

Jack stared at it, trying to make out some kind of pattern. There was none. One had been a lone male in a residential urban alley; the other had been a gang of youths in the most deserted area of the local park. He let out a sigh, wishing his instincts would come up with some avenue of investigation.

"What about the lad, Sullivan?" Jack asked.

"He has been sectioned and was taken to hospital this morning," the DI told him. "He was climbing the walls, screaming that the dogs that attacked his friends were going to come after him. He's lost it big time."

"The only dogs in the park were the Oscar Zero unit. The handlers insist they were not let off the leads at all, and frankly, with the time frame, there was no way two dogs could have done that kind of damage, run back to the handlers, got back on their leads and cleared away all traces of blood."

"Well, that dog unit has been taken off the road anyway," Andrea said.

"What!" Jack exclaimed. "Why?"

Andrea shrugged. "You know what this job is like; the powers that be want to cover themselves, so the dogs are being investigated in case they did get a bit enthusiastic."

"That's a load of bollocks! There is no way they're to blame."

Jack sighed again, knowing it was pointless to argue when everyone in the room agreed with him. He leaned against one of the desks and looked at the floor. He was left without a suspect and without any way forward. All he could do now was hope the public appeal came up with some witnesses.

"What if there's another one tonight?" Jack asked.

"The chief super has authorised another firearms unit to come on division and be on standby. I think he's a little spooked."

"More than one firearms unit. Isn't that a bit drastic?"

DI Sprite nodded. "Well, TSG didn't do much good, did it?"

Sunday afternoon, 1400 hours

Jack leaned forward in the seat of the unmarked car he was driving as the massive wrought-iron gates opened slowly. Andrea, in the seat next to him, let out a sound of wonder as the car rolled forward along the gravel driveway of the mansion. It was about half a mile long and bordered on either side by thick, dense woodland that opened up to reveal a spacious park and beautiful, stately home of the sort one would expect to be featured on an antiques show.

Jack followed the directions to the visitors car park and pulled up, noting that they were not the only guests there this day. He and Andrea got out, and he heard her make a noise of approval at the tall, young black man who came over to them, a warm expression on his face.

"Hello there," he said, shaking them both by the hand. "I am Ms Harper's personal assistant, Stefan."

Jack made the introductions and then followed Stefan as he led them round the edge of the house.

"So this place is a zoo as well?" Jack asked.

Stefan nodded and pointed to a high concrete wall in the distance. "Yes, it's over there. We keep it separate from the estate. Did you know the zoo also holds an animal hospital?"

Andrea nodded. "I came here with my kids last year. They loved the butterfly house."

Stefan smiled at her. "Did they get to have the butterflies on their arms?" he asked. Andrea smiled, and Stefan continued. "We do try to encourage as much contact as we can so that children learn to respect the animal kingdom. Did you see the farm as well?"

Again the DC nodded. "I didn't realise that Moonscape Inc. owned all of this."

"This and several other projects around the world. Ms Harper also has some charities and causes close to her heart."

Stefan walked ahead of them, and as his feet trod the gravel walkway, Jack was aware of the sheer size of the man. He was huge; he looked as though he lived in the gym and could have bench-pressed a tank. The way the man walked could only be described as stalking, and even though his feet touched the ground, it seemed as though he was making noise deliberately.

They came to a gate fixed in a brick wall that had a massive sign on it denying entry. Stefan opened the gate and stood aside to let the officers in.

Immediately, Jack became aware of the sound of barking. Not just one dog, either, but loads. He could see tall, spacious cages everywhere and a fenced-off play area as big as a football field. In this play area was a pack of about forty dogs, all barking, jumping, and playing around a woman whom he recognised from the website. She was wearing a black tracksuit and had bright pink hair, and she held aloft a ball in one hand.

At the sight of the ball, the dogs became frantic and backed away from her, tensing as they waited. She pulled back her arm and let fly. Jack was impressed at the throw and saw all the dogs tear off after it, trying to catch it.

Some of the dogs raced off to the pool and dove in, splashing about in pure delight. Jack looked at Andrea and saw she had her phone out and was filming the whole thing. She met his look.

"What? I watch her show all the time!" she said.

Jack shook his head. "If you ever take the piss out of me watching *Haunted Britain*, I'm going to remind you of this."

Victoria turned away from the dogs, nodded to a young female assistant, and ran over to a sheltered area which housed a sink. She washed and dried her hands quickly and then approached the two detectives.

"Hello, I'm Vicky Harper. You must be Detective Sergeant Ladd and Detective Bowman. Pleased to meet you," she said, shaking hands.

Jack could always tell a suspect by their greeting. Some were arrogant and shook hands in order to press their luck; others avoided all contact as though that would reveal their guilt. This woman seemed to be a very confident individual, but he could tell she was extremely nervous around him. Most people got that way around police, and it did not mean anything, but Jack had learned to sense when someone disliked his profession in the same way that women were able to pick out the creep in the bar.

He smiled at her as they shook hands and wanted to put her at ease. She was, after all, only a slight person of interest and not a serious contender on the suspect list.

Once the pleasantries were done, Victoria led them into the mansion and towards the left wing. She showed them into a massive wood-panelled office which overlooked the rear grounds of the estate. Jack took in the details of the room quickly. There were photographs of Victoria lining the walls from recent times to years ago, each one featuring a different world leader or celebrity. One particular photo caught his interest. He recognised it from somewhere. It was a floral display in the shape of the word *women* in front of a tree. Attached to the wall underneath the photo was a banner in purple, white, and green.

Again it was strangely familiar to him, but he could not for the life of him remember where he had seen it before.

Victoria showed him to the two sofas at one end of the office. Tea had been placed on the low dark wood and glass table. Seated on one of the sofas was Marcus. He seemed to unfold rather than stand and introduced himself to Jack and Andrea. Behind Marcus stood Ingrid.

Jack had not realised they would have such an audience. Stefan served the tea as they all sat down, apart from Ingrid, whom Jack could have sworn was sizing him up for her dinner table.

"So, how can I help you?" Victoria asked.

Andrea let out a giggle. Jack frowned at her, and she had the decency to look contrite. "I'm so sorry. I do apologise – it's just that I watch your programme all the time, Ms Harper, and I never thought I'd hear that phrase in person."

Victoria laughed, and Marcus felt her relax. "Yes, I guess that is a phrase I use quite often." She shrugged her shoulders and raised her hands slightly. "Well, how can I help you?"

Jack was perched on the edge of his seat. In his hands he held a folder. "You have heard about the murders in the town centre and Beachwood Park?"

Both Victoria and Marcus nodded.

"Unfortunately, it is looking more and more like an animal attack."

He waited for his statement to sink in and gage their reactions.

Marcus shrugged his shoulders. "So most of the news programmes and the papers have been saying."

"Well, as you have a private zoo and the dog sanctuary here, we need to question you about security in case any of the animals escaped."

"Of course, we will be more than happy to help," Marcus said. "Although I can tell you now, none of the animals have escaped. We have CCTV on them at all times, and our security is top level."

"We will need verification of that."

Ingrid stepped forward. "As head of security, I'd be more than happy to show you all CCTV."

Jack stared at her. "I'd need to get a couple of units here to go through it ourselves."

"That will not be a problem, Sergeant. Moonscape has nothing to hide," Marcus said.

Jack nodded to Andrea. "DC Bowman will liaise with your head of security and arrange for a unit to join us."

Andrea stood up. "I'll need to look at it now myself though."

Ingrid nodded and raised her arm. "No problem. Please come with me."

Victoria watched the young detective constable leave. She was surprised that the woman was so normal for a police officer. She was professional, no doubt about that, and obviously a fan of hers, and she looked at her surroundings with a sense of awe. Victoria made a note to offer her a guided tour, and she found herself on unusual ground. These two officers were not what she had expected.

The detective sergeant was fascinated by his surroundings, but he was very quick and polite about it. He was also very observant of the people around him and their reactions to his questions and statements. He was definitely scrutinising both her and Marcus, and he did not trust them. She could also tell that he had been at the last murder scene just after it had happened. Not only could she smell the flesh and blood, but she could detect the stink of the rogue pack on him.

"Sergeant, are you completely sure this is the work of animals?" she asked.

Jack nodded. "After last night, yes. I was one of the first on scene, but one of our officers used to work in the morgue and compared both scenes to a lion attack in another zoo last year."

Marcus made a noise. "Oh, the one where the handler decided to enter the enclosure whilst they were feeding?" He shook his head. "We have had lions from cubs, hand reared them in the mansion, but never, ever would any of us go in the enclosure whilst they eat. Big mistake."

Jack had to smile at the echo of Brett's words, and he felt a little relieved. Instinct told him they did not have anything to do with the murders, but he was still careful. "Would you mind if I showed you some photos?" he asked.

He opened the folder at her nod of agreement and handed her the copies of the crime scene photos. She gave just the right reaction of disgust and horror at them but composed herself well; she had obviously seen similar before. Victoria examined them and then handed them over to Marcus.

"My husband and I used to travel to Kenya on safari. Some of the poachers would murder tourists and leave their remains for the animals to finish off." She took a breath. "It has been many years since I have seen a human body in that state, but one never forgets."

Marcus handed the photos back. "Yes, Sergeant. Your officer was right; that does look like an animal attack."

"Could dogs do that?" Jack asked.

Victoria thought about it. "Depends if that is what they are trained to do. No dog will attack a human unless it is in danger or trained to. This could be an attack pack."

"What about feral dogs?"

She shook her head vehemently. "Absolutely not. They tend to stay away from humans. If he were dead already, then perhaps. This was definitely, in my professional opinion, a pack of dogs who have been trained to do this. There is a big problem with dog fighting in this area that I have been trying to stop. I've been working with the council to hunt down and stop these gangs; however, they are very good at shutting down their operations quickly and leaving no trace."

Jack took the information in and sighed. Gangs running fighting dog rings were just another complication he did not need in this case.

Sunday afternoon, 1600 hours

Marcus watched the police unit pull into the car park of the security building. The two uniformed officers got out along with a plain-clothes detective. He was apparently the CCTV expert and would be going through all the surveillance cameras and hopefully eliminating them from the enquiries.

Ingrid had ordered her people to be open and honest with the officers and allow them full access to the CCTV from the zoo and the dog sanctuary. Marcus had smiled at the specific and deliberate instructions. The mansion and the pack areas were not included.

He allowed himself a little relief. Pack exposure would now be reduced to a minimum, and they had the one responsible for making the rogue pack in custody. An omega, no less, one who was incredibly low in the hierarchy of the pack, and Marcus was stunned that he had managed to hide it so well. Any further potential damage could be limited. The rogues themselves still needed to be dealt with; they were all guilty of murder and could not go unpunished.

Marcus had requested nine of the alphas from pack branches around the world to come to the mansion. It was one of the tasks of an alpha to reprimand serious offences, and making a rogue pack was one of those. As soon as the criminal had been brought in by Ingrid, Marcus had made the phone calls, and the others were now en route.

Marcus watched the three officers disappear into the security building, and then he turned and walked back into the mansion. He made his way to the expansive kitchens and towards the door leading down to the cellars. The cavernous rooms that comprised the cellars were dark and stretched over the entire area of the mansion; the main part of them was used for storing the wide and expensive collection of wines, most of which had been collected by his father.

He approached a steel door at the end of the wine cellars and punched a code into the state-of-the-art security keypad. The door clicked open quietly, and Marcus stepped into the enclosure.

Lights shone brightly in the white hallway, and the air conditioning hummed quietly as the door closed behind him. He was greeted by the sound of laughter coming from one of the many well-appointed rooms off the corridor. He poked his head into this room and exchanged greetings with the teenagers who sat on the large stuffed sofa playing on a games console. There were two girls and one boy, all of whom had now reached the age of the Change.

The Change always came to a born wolf during puberty, and for the first few months of transformation, they spent the week of each full moon at the mansion, safe, secure, and free to learn how to control it without the fear of harming outsiders unintentionally.

The girls bragged about beating their male friend at a war game, which made Marcus grin; they obviously wanted to be trained by Ingrid when old enough. He made sure they had everything they needed and then made his way to the cages.

They were cages by name, and that was their purpose, but they were not cells in the traditional sense of the word. They were rooms, comfortable but basic, each with a small bed fixed into the wall. With steel and concrete walls that were several feet thick and doors that would have made any bank manager weep with envy, each room provided a safe haven for Change.

New pack members and new Changers slept here and learned the control needed in order to survive the modern world. Marcus's father had pioneered the new methods of transformation and learned that if a young wolf, made or born, was allowed to Change intensely and frequently in a secure environment, he or she gained better control, learned to change more quickly, and avoided accidental transformations in public. Thus the myth of the werewolf had faded into Hollywood and pop culture.

Marcus came to the last and most secure cage, which was hardly ever used and was reserved for those the pack considered criminals. It was larger, with no bed and only one chair.

Robin sat on this chair. He was not bound by any physical restraints, but he remained there just the same. His head was bowed, and Marcus could smell the blood that dripped from the countless cuts and grazes he now sported.

Ingrid stood by the table she had had moved into the room. Her suit jacket was folded neatly on top of it next to a first-aid kit, and she sipped water from a pink sports bottle. Her shirt was pristine, her blonde hair still neatly pulled back in an immaculate ponytail. The only indications of her efforts were the grazes on her knuckles, which were healing even as Marcus approached her.

"Any luck?" Marcus asked.

Ingrid glanced at Robin. "No, boss. Tosser won't say anything to me. I've been at him on and off since I brought him in. I was about to grab some silver spray," she replied.

Robin whimpered from where he sat and looked up at them helplessly.

Marcus watched Robin. "Why don't you go and get our guest some food, Ingrid."

Ingrid nodded and picked up her suit jacket. She left the room, and Marcus closed the door softly behind her. He padded over to the table where the first-aid kit sat and took out some antiseptic wipes. He then walked over to Robin and squatted in front of him.

Robin jerked away as Marcus lifted his hand and then relaxed a little as the pack alpha began to clean his cuts and grazes gently, tenderly.

"Little Robin Simmons." Marcus sighed. "I remember watching you play on the grounds when you were a child. Always so full of fun and laughter."

Robin watched cautiously as Marcus stood up and replaced the wipes.

"You will heal, Robin. Ingrid can be a bit harsh at times," he said.

Robin tried to block out his voice; it was so smooth, so gentle and seductive, but it cut through him with each syllable uttered.

"Why, Robin? Why did you do this thing?" Marcus asked, making his voice a whisper.

Marcus knelt down beside Robin and began to stroke his head tenderly. Robin felt the wolf inside him roll. Marcus was his alpha, and Robin had to obey him.

Robin began to cry. "I wanted my own pack," he sniffed.

"But Robin, you had your own pack. You had us."

"No! I wanted to be an alpha!" Robin wailed, letting his anger and sense of injustice show. "All I am is your omega, low ranking. I deserve more."

Marcus shushed him and continued to stroke his head. "I know, I know," he soothed. "What went wrong, Robin?"

Robin heaved his breath in. "One of them was an alpha. He took them from me. I only wanted to help them. They were addicts and had no bonds!"

Marcus nodded. "You wanted them to feel what it is like to be pack, to have the unity and the bond." Robin looked at him. "I understand, but you did not intend for this murder to happen. You have to tell us where they are."

Robin shook his head. "I cannot. I made them."

Marcus stood up and looked down at Robin. "You poor, poor misguided creature. You are an omega, that is true, but not without worth. I have watched you grow. You went to the best schools, university, all paid for by the pack. I saw you develop a gift of perception and counselling – so much so that your words sounded like magic to all who heard them." Marcus nodded. "Yes, omega you may be, but you had been my first choice for head counsellor – the wolf present at the first Change of each new wolf, helping them, guiding them into the life."

Robin looked up at Marcus, disbelief haunting his heart. He knew what that meant. Every young wolf around the world would have been under his care. It was an incredible badge of honour, a position of extreme privilege.

"Every member of the pack was asked about this role. All mentioned your name, Robin. You are omega, but you were loved and respected."

You *were* loved and respected. The past tense was not lost on Robin.

Marcus sighed. "You now have a decision to make, Robin," he continued. "You have been directly responsible for the murder of innocent people, and that carries a sentence of death. Out of respect for your father, I give you this offer: run the alpha gauntlet with one month banishment, or face life-long expulsion from the pack."

Robin choked.

"Yes, Robin. You will live out your days alone, denied the family you have betrayed and put in danger. No member of the pack will speak to you, give you shelter, or acknowledge you in any way. None of the sanctuaries will be open to you, and from this day you will be dead to all of us. We will not see you," Marcus promised, his voice becoming more definite as he spoke.

Robin swallowed. "Eighty-four Lilly Court," he whispered. "I choose the gauntlet."

Marcus nodded. "Thank you, Robin," he said. "I'll have Ingrid move you to a proper cage."

Marcus opened the door and stepped out into the corridor. Ingrid stood waiting with a tray of food and a glass of water. She grinned at Marcus triumphantly.

CHAPTER SEVEN

Sunday evening, 1900 hours

Ingrid stared at the mouth of the alley and the two PCSOs who were still standing on the cordon. She smirked as she overheard their conversation about how cold they were, which was punctuated with polite exchanges with passers-by. She stood by her van, her suit jacket back on, and was very glad that the cold weather did not affect her. Winter was definitely on the way though; she could smell the frost in the air.

James looked at her from the driver's seat of the van, and Ingrid could sense the question in his stare. They had the address. They should be going there and not hanging around a crime scene they had already sniffed out.

Ingrid smiled as she heard the footsteps coming up from behind. She turned to face the newcomer. "You're getting better at sneaking up on the pack," she said.

"Good to hear," the female said.

"Have you got your silver darts with you?" Ingrid asked.

The woman nodded. "Yep, I'm going to stash them in my locker along with my silver knife."

"Lot of bloody good they'll do you in there, love! You must keep them on you at all times!"

"I can't carry those weapons at work!" the woman exclaimed.

"These rogues are not pack. They will kill you without thinking twice about it," Ingrid pointed out.

The woman looked at her evenly, unafraid. "So what are you doing about it? If we catch any of them, what then?"

"We are dealing with it," Ingrid said.

"Well, message from my dad: either you deal with it, or we will," the woman said.

Ingrid met her eyes. "I said we are dealing with it. I agreed to meet with you to tell you that."

"My dad is calling in every hunter he knows, not to mention that I've spoken to people about DS Ladd. He's really good at what he does. He could probably smell a suspect better than you can."

Ingrid gave a short laugh. "I've met him; he's not too bad for a human."

The woman sighed and then handed Ingrid a piece of paper. "This is the information you wanted about the address you gave me. If anything else happens, I'll let you know. Now all of that is my information that I've picked up from other people. I am not getting sacked for looking stuff up I shouldn't be."

Ingrid unfolded the paperwork and looked at the handwritten information on the inside. She giggled. "It's a house you will want to wipe your feet on the way out of," she read. "Ta, love. Keep you and yours safe, OK?"

The woman nodded and began to walk away. "Yep, and I'll so kick your arse at the gym Friday night. I'm in need of good work out!"

Sunday night, 2000 hours

James parked the van outside the address Robin had given them and shut off the engine. Ingrid got out of the passenger side and looked at the small terraced house in front of her.

Apparently, this area of the borough was one of the most run down, and she could feel the destitution. She could feel the poverty of the area all around her and could feel eyes watching her. The stares did not bother her; she was way more dangerous than any of these drunk or drugged-up wasters whose only desire in life was a benefit cheque. Her lip curled with distaste. Free loaders were not allowed in the pack; everyone contributed in some way, and everyone was looked after as a result. Sometimes, the rule of the animal kingdom was a good thing.

Their contact had been right; the house was filthy beyond belief. Ingrid was going to have to have a very long hot shower when she had finished. How had Robin tolerated living in such disgusting conditions? They had not even entered the house yet, and the smell wafted out to them like a cloud.

James stood beside her, along with Max and Vanessa. They were the best of her security officers, and she did not want to take any chances. From the research she had done after Robin spilled his guts, this pack were essentially a bunch of junkies. They had gone from being on drugs to being wolves, and that was not a good transition.

Behaviour traits followed someone Bitten. A strong, secure, person became a vital member of the pack. However, if there were any psychosis, any trauma emotionally, anger issues, or addiction, then those traits followed and were magnified. This explained why Robin had lost control of the pack he had made and why they were on a killing spree.

"Right then, let's go," Ingrid ordered.

Max and Vanessa nodded in compliance and made their way to the rear of the property. Ingrid and James waited at the front, and when their colleagues were in position, a faint growl wafted on the air to them. It was a pack signal, and no one – not even a rogue wolf – would pick up on it.

Ingrid trotted up the path to the front door, James at her back as always. As she neared the front door, she noticed that it was ajar. Signalling the others to keep an eye out, Ingrid softly pushed open the door and stepped inside.

The smell of drugs hit her, and as she looked around, she saw all manner of paraphernalia, including a crack pipe and some flame-stained spoons. She shook her head at the sheer waste of it all and then looked around the shabby, dirty property.

It was empty save for drugs and the finished bottles of booze. Gas, electric, and water had been shut off, and she could tell that they had been squatting in it. The smell of urine and faeces was strong, and again she marvelled at the waste. These wolves knew nothing of how to be, well, wolves.

She shook her head. "It's no good. They're long gone," she said. "Dammit!"

Monday morning, 1000 hours

Mike "Howling Wolf" McLeary stood in front of the full-length mirror and brushed out his waist-long black hair until it shone like silk. He was tall for one of the People of the Wolf but moved his lithe, muscular frame with an easy grace.

He moved to the dresser and fastened his watch to his wrist. He had been the first of the alphas to arrive in the early hours and had taken the chance to doze and ease his body clock into British time.

Marcus had called him the day before, and Mike had left the reservation and told his staff to prepare the jet immediately. He knew that the other Alphas were en route too; this was a situation that had to be addressed immediately.

Mike smiled as he heard the padding of paws behind him and turned to the open doorway. He clapped his hands and braced himself as Dace yipped and ran over to him, big pink tongue lolling out.

Mike ended up on the floor, rolling around with the Husky. He grabbed the dog by the face and placed his forehead on the dog's snout.

"Hello, Inuit brother," he whispered.

Mike then stood up and followed Dace out of the guest bedroom and down to the kitchen.

Marcus and Victoria were sat at the kitchen table, and both looked up as Mike walked in. Victoria walked over to him and hugged him tightly.

"Mike, it is good to see you again," she said.

"Except this time I am visiting as an alpha," he said. "My father now walks with the sky spirits."

Marcus shook his hand and hugged him. "I know. When did he pass?"

Mike smiled. "A while back. He chose to leave this realm as wolf and was in the sanctuary for months before he died."

Marcus smiled. "A good way to leave. We have several elders in the wolf section at the moment. They are well looked after."

Mike poured a coffee from the machine and sat at the table. He fixed Marcus with his black eyes. "How bad is it?"

Marcus sat opposite him. "You've seen the news? You know about the murders?" he asked. Mike nodded. "That's the rogue pack Robin made. That has now been confirmed."

"Robin Simmons? Why?" Mike asked.

Marcus shrugged. "He wanted to be an alpha of his own pack. He believed he was better than omega with us."

"So we could be exposed," Mike said quietly.

"There may be no way to stop it now. With the media and the social networking the way it is now, if they are arrested, they will reveal themselves. That is inevitable, as it seems they are only a month old, wolf wise. Once they are unmasked, eventually, by association, so will we be."

"We need a business plan then, so we can adapt. This is why you summoned the rest of us, not just for the gauntlet."

Marcus nodded. "Jacques may use this to challenge me. He has been looking for an excuse for years, and I cannot say I blame him."

"If he dares to, he will be on his own; the rest of us will back you, Marcus."

"But it is a thread, Mike. He will use this and worry it until the whole fabric falls apart." He sighed. "No, my wolf brother, everything is about to change for us."

Mike remembered a story his grandfather had told him of when he was young. He had been curious as to why, of all the People, they were still on their land, and why the white man had not taken it from them. His grandfather had barked a laugh, sitting by his fire in the wooden hut he lived in, and had told him of their wolf brothers.

His grandfather was a boy at the time, and his grandfather's grandfather was chief of the tribe. They had heard about their human brothers being forced off of land they had roamed for hundreds of years because the white man could not slake his hunger for that which was not his. The People of the Wolf listened in horror as the stories reached them of the atrocities committed against the People, of the rape and the murder, of the wars and the battles that ensued to no avail. The chief made a choice to execute any white man who entered their land.

Wolf hunters came, seeking the beasts that felled the scouts, and the tribe retreated father into the land. The white men turned back at the first winter in this the most extreme of environments, and the Wolf People were jubilant. The white men were nothing to nature, because they did not know how to respect it.

In the darkest of winter, a lone white male crossed into the land. The scouts watched him but did not attack, for he would be dead soon enough. He wore only light clothing, carried a pack containing very little, and seemed to have nothing to help him endure the snow. When the first blizzard came, the scouts waited. The tall blonde man walked from the storm unaffected and continued towards the camp.

This was no ordinary white man.

As he neared the camp day by day, he was observed. He seemed to have a reverence for the world around him. They lost sight of him when he hunted the deer, but he did not waste any portion of the beast – very unusual for a white man. Every night at his campfire, the scouts saw him take a leather-wrapped package from his pack and hold it reverently to his chest, muttering.

Eventually he reached the camp and he stopped. He did not enter the camp, but he took up position just outside, sat on the snow-covered ground, crossed his legs, and waited.

The chief was curious because of the reports of this white male and went out to meet him. His young grandson accompanied the old man. They approached the man, who had not moved, and stood before him. His long blonde hair and beard were caked with ice and snow, but he did not shiver. In front of him sat the leather package.

As the chief stood there, the white male looked up at him with eyes so blue that they glowed like the sky on a summer's day. "I am Siguard Ulf," he said in the language of the People, his name sounding harsh.

The chief did not say anything. The white man then took off his shirt, and the shocked mutterings of the people could be heard, stunned that he would be doing this in such cold weather.

The white man extended an arm, closed his eyes, and went very still. The chief watched in avid curiosity. The arm rippled, and then there was the unmistakable sound of cracking bones. The skin pulsed and throbbed, the fingers broke and became claws, and hair sprouted thickly over exposed skin. The man then opened his eyes, the blue of them shimmering in the daylight, and as he opened his mouth to speak, his fangs were visible.

"Everything is about to change, my wolf brother, and I am here to help you …"

Mike looked at the small golden bowl he had brought with him. It was battered and dented, with stains from long years of use. This fine gift was a symbol between his ancestor and Marcus's. Their wolf brother had bought their land and returned it to the people. They now owned it by the white man's rules and found the gift a great boon.

Other tribes sought sanctuary, and the Wolf People gave it with open arms, and they thrived, protected by the white law and able to survive.

Mike poured the expensive scotch whiskey into the bowl. Now his people were rich and powerful in their native land ruled by the white man. Profits had boomed over the last forty years, as some of the white men now appreciated nature and paid for the honour of seeing it first-hand. Their wolf-watching tours were some of the best in the world, not to mention the hiking, climbing, and camping grounds they ran. In aiding the Wolf People, Siguard had ensured them wealth both material and cultural.

Mike turned to Marcus and offered him the bowl. The younger man took it in both hands and drank deeply.

"To family," he whispered and handed the bowl back.

"To family," Mike echoed, and drank.

Monday night, 2100 hours

"Both crime scenes are still open, and we will need people to stand on them, as the PCSOs can't work past midnight," Inspector Kent began. "Luckily, duties have authorised overtime, so we have a few more units on than usual. Firearms have given us two units for the foreseeable future, and the chief superintendent is upstairs listening in on the radio, so watch what you say."

She looked over the crowded parade room. "All units on the street are to observe the risk assessment. I don't want anybody out there single-crewed, and if that means you triple up, so be it. All of you are to wear body armour, no exceptions."

"Is there anything more on the murders, guv?" Andrew asked.

Inspector Kent gave a wry grin. "Well, there haven't been any more murders, so far. The murder squad are leaning towards a pack of fighting dogs instructed to do this by someone. Possibly a drug dealer who hasn't come to our attention yet. As you know, the famous Vicky Harper is advising them on dog psychology and giving them the info she has on dog fighting rings in the area. Other than that, there are no updates."

"What about Jack Sullivan?" Brett asked. "Has he said anything more?"

"He is still at the local hospital being treated for severe shock," she told him.

"At least he isn't out robbing anymore," Pete muttered.

"Somehow I don't think he will be doing that in a hurry. He saw what was left of his friends," Lauren told him.

"Back to other news," the inspector went on. "Tonight there is a late licence at Cannons Bar. There will be a lot of people there, so be prepared for any fighting."

Pete clapped his hands together and rubbed them gleefully. "I am so glad I get to go out and play tonight," he said.

Lauren laughed. "Will you be using the home-office-approved sitting on your suspect move?" she asked.

He gave her an even stare. "It's in the same manual as your ankle biting manoeuvre," he retorted.

"Now, now, children," Liv chided. "Play nice together."

Inspector Kent indicated one of the pictures pinned onto the board behind her. It was of a short, blonde-haired, blue-eyed man who looked pale and drawn. "We all know Matthew Westmore. He is a known drug addict and burglar. He was imprisoned for GBH with intent and was released two months ago on probation." There were mumbles and huffs from the seated officers. "I know; it's a joke. We should have been told about this ages ago, but the paperwork for him wasn't sent to us by his drugs worker. Punchline is that he spent most of his sentence in hospital."

"I hope it was something serious," Andrew commented.

"He was suffering from some kind of psychological disorder. One of his bail conditions is to attend the local mental health wing at the hospital once a week for treatment."

"Care in the community works its magic once more," Pete put in.

"What is he suffering from?" Brett asked.

Inspector Kent looked over her clipboard. "Er, a condition called lycanthropy."

Lauren sat up quickly. "Lycanthropy? Guv, are you sure?"

She nodded. "That's what it says here. Why?"

"Do you know what that is?" Lauren asked.

The inspector shook her head.

"Lycanthropy is a disorder where the sufferer believes they are a werewolf."

There was a moment of silence as Lauren waited for everyone to get what it was she was driving at. Liv's eyes widened, and she turned pale, but she did not speak.

"What has that got to do with anything?" Andrew asked.

Lauren looked at him. "The murders?" she said as though he should have known. "We all know how violent Matthew got when he was out of his head on drugs. If he really does believe he turns into a werewolf, and he is still on the drugs, he could be capable of anything."

Andrew screwed up his face in disbelief. "What, rip apart all those people, even those kids, and make it look like a wild animal did it?"

Lauren shrugged and nodded. "Yeah, if he was high enough. When he was arrested by us one time, it took eight TSG officers to hold him down, and even then it was hard enough."

Inspector Kent looked at Lauren squarely. "How do you know about this condition?"

"I watch a lot of horror movies, plus my dad studied it."

"Could Matthew be doing this on his own?"

"I don't know, guv. People who suffer from lycanthropy are usually loners, but Matthew's old druggie gang are still around. He may be staying with one of them."

Inspector Kent made a few notes on her clipboard. "I want you to go and tell the murder squad this. Some of them are still up in CID. At this time they could use any information we have."

Lauren nodded and then listened to the rest of the briefing. It was just the usual tasking list and another reminder to keep an eye on Cannons Bar. There was always a fight there; the place had become well known for it.

As the room cleared, Lauren's mobile phone began to ring. She walked along the corridor next to Brett as she held it to her ear.

"Hello, it's only me," Kenny's voice said.

Lauren tried not to blush. "What are you doing, calling me here?" she asked, trying to sound neutral.

Brett held the back door open for her and gave her a curious stare; she did not meet his gaze.

"I've got something to tell you, my sweet," Kenny told her.

"Oh, what?"

"Are you sitting down?" he asked.

She ran down the steps. "I'm just about to pick up my car. Of course not."

"Oh well." Kenny sighed. "I'm letting you know that I'm going back out with Jackie."

Lauren stopped and felt the blood drain from her cheeks. Brett was staring at her, as were the other members of her team. She forced herself to smile. Everything was normal.

"Are you happy for me?" Kenny asked.

Of course not, you arrogant bastard, Lauren wanted to tell him, but with so many eyes on her, she kept control. "Of course," she lied, the strain of it shaking her voice.

"Great!" he said. "What I'll do is call you in a few weeks' time, and we can all go out for a meal."

"Will she be all right with that?" Lauren asked in surprise.

"Of course. She knew I was seeing you. I told her after we split up that we were going out."

"Oh. I'll see what I'm up to." She shook her head and felt a pulling in her stomach. "I've got to go. Bye."

"Goodbye, my sweet."

She hung up on him and looked around the yard, feeling her heart thunder in her ears.

Pete stood by the van, all kitted out with belt and Met vest, leaning against it casually, looking at her with a huge grin on his face. "Was that this mysterious boyfriend of yours?" he asked. "Are you going to tell us who he is then?"

"Don't bother, Pete. I've been trying to get a name for the last few weeks," Brett said.

Lauren forced out a laugh. "For that, you two can do my checks whilst I go to the loo and then see CID."

Lauren trotted back into the building and ran up to the ladies' room on the second floor near the CID office. She shut herself in one of the cubicles and began to shake uncontrollably. She felt a sharp pain rip at her insides and then began to throw up into the bowl.

When she had finished retching, she dabbed at her clammy, pale face with a damp tissue. Then, after a drink of water, she walked calmly from the toilet and went into CID.

CHAPTER EIGHT

Monday night, 2200 hours

Amy was pissed off. She stormed out of the house in a huff after finding out that he had gone out without her again. He had done it more and more in the last few days, and she hated not knowing where he was going or what he was doing.

At first, when he had got out two months ago and headed straight for her bedsit, it had been great, just like old times when they used to drink, get high, and then screw each other's brains out. She had been put on a drugs programme after social services took her second child away, and he had to attend the same meetings, but they were together again, and she loved it.

Amy was only seventeen years old but felt a lot older. For as long as she could remember, the world had been against her – even her own mother, who had given up on her at the age of ten. She was put in the care of social services after her younger brother had kept her up all night and she had tried to keep him quiet. Her anger had got the better of her, but no one saw that his constant wailing was wrong, and when he had choked it had not been her fault; she had just been holding his mouth shut to teach him that crying was not allowed.

Then there was the time when she saw those new slip-on shoes all the girls in her class had. She asked her mum for a pair and was refused. Was it not her job to feed and clothe her? Why else had the old cow had a child? Amy was angry with her mum, and just as she had been punished as a child, she punished the woman for not looking after her. Her mum was on the phone to police, and Amy ripped it from her hand and used it to smack her. Her mum sent Amy to her room, and that really made her mad; she wanted to smash everything and grabbed the nearest thing and threw it at her. The hot cup of tea scalded her mum, and when police turned up, she was taken away.

Amy had her first boyfriend at eleven, and at twelve she had her first baby, and she was taken away from her. Her boyfriend was two years older and lived in the same children's home, and he was taken away too. She went out and got pregnant again, because who were the social to say that she was not allowed to have a baby?

Now Amy was different, and she wanted that social worker to pay. That old woman had written a report saying, "Amy should never be left alone in a room with a child, baby, or any living creature." What a cow! She was going to pay for that, Amy was certain, and now she had the means to do it.

The drugs were great, but they were on the substitutes while under the care of the local drugs workers. Group therapy was so boring, but at least meeting the others was good. Inderjit, Craig, and Thomas were friends of Matthew's, and they had all lived in the same squat together, but she had only ever seen them in passing before they partied.

Then one day during a session their drugs worker had come up with a new therapy and an idea that had completely wowed them all. Now she was powerful, strong, and did not like the drugs anymore. No, there was something better, and it came in the form of hunting those people who had done her wrong and making them pay, very slowly.

Matthew had been all for that idea too. It was amazing how strong he was and how he had taken charge of everything. She had never seen him like this, and she loved it. Even that stupid drugs worker who had changed them was not as strong as her man. Matthew had his own list of people he wanted to get even with, as did the others, and as they started to pick off their targets, they got better at it and more confident.

Amy wanted to start on her list of people, but Matthew refused, saying he had not finished his yet. She was not happy and told him so. He did not care about how she felt, and he started going out on his own. He was her man, and he was not allowed to do that. So she left the house with Craig and went looking for him. Maybe she could make Craig her boyfriend and teach Matthew a lesson. If he became jealous, then it was his own fault and not hers.

Amy stopped outside the convenience store near to the High Street. It was a post office and an off licence too, so it was still open. She could smell that Matthew had been in there not long ago, and she wandered in with Craig following behind.

The Indian store owner had known her for years and called out a greeting to her. Matthew had always used this shop to cash his benefit and buy his booze, and she had tagged along with him most of the time. Recently, having got the credit card and PIN number from the drugs worker, they had bought a lot of drink with lots of cash. In the current economy, the store owner never questioned how they came by so much money, and they did not tell.

She walked up to the counter and smiled at the owner. "Have you seen Matthew tonight?" she asked.

The store owner nodded. "He was in about half an hour ago," he said in a heavy Indian accent. "He said he was off to the High Street."

Amy nodded and then looked up at the television screen on the wall behind the cash register. The news was on and she saw CCTV footage of herself. It was a blur, but she knew it was her.

Amy grabbed Craig's arm and jumped up and down in excitement. "Look, Craig! It's me! I'm on telly!"

Craig giggled and hung on to her. The store owner looked at the footage and realised it was the murder and she was pointing to herself as the blonde suspect. His hand reached for the phone, but quick as a flash, she reached out and grabbed his wrist.

He winced at the pain, astonished by her strength, and looked into her furious, glowing eyes. Licking his lips nervously, he smiled at her, trying to put her at ease.

Amy let him go and took two steps back. "You fucking wanker!" she yelled.

She then turned back to the shop floor and started to kick at the shelves in the middle. They toppled and smashed, jars and bottles shattering on the floor. The owner took cover behind the counter as she screamed her fury and ripped everything down, destroying as much as she could. She then hurled wine bottles behind the counter, and he shielded himself as glass and liquid showered down on him.

Then all was quiet. Cautiously, he raised his head and peeked over the counter top. The shop was empty; both Amy and Craig had gone.

PC Sam Buchanan parked the car and got out, followed by Andrew. They walked up to the ruined shop and took cautious steps in, their boots crunching on the glass.

The store owner was behind the counter, talking rapidly in Punjabi to another man, arms waving around in the air frantically. Both men turned to the police officers and started to shout at them, their voices growing higher and more incomprehensible.

Andrew frowned and tried to calm the victims. Sam just gave a strange little smile.

"Look, gentlemen, why don't you take a deep breath and tell me what happened," he said in flawless Punjabi.

Andrew blinked at Sam, and the two Indian men looked stunned.

The next twenty minutes were spent with Andrew looking confused as Sam spoke to the victims in their own language and wrote everything down in his pocketbook. Both men looked decidedly relieved as Sam nodded sympathetically with them. He then spoke to them again, handing out a small card with details on it. Some phrases Andrew recognised, such as "CID" and "crime reference number", but the rest of it went over his head.

Sam walked out onto the street and called CID on his radio. "Hi there, it's three-six-four here," he began. "You'll need to come and speak to the owners of the Quality Food Store on Fairfax Street. It seems the blonde woman from the CCTV was here and they know her. Her name is Amy Farringdon."

The night duty CID officers thanked him, and Sam looked at Andrew. "What?" he asked in response to the stare from the probationer.

"You speak Punjabi?" Andrew said incredulously.

Sam nodded. "Punjabi, Urdu, Hindi, and a little Farsi and Arabic," he said and then laughed at Andrew. "My Granny was from India and used to take care of me when I was a kid," he explained.

Andrew took in Sam's dark blonde hair and grey eyes. "But—"

"I don't look Indian?" Sam finished. He shrugged his shoulders. "Granny married a Scott. I'm about a quarter Indian. Just wait till the last night duty, and if I can, I'll be making the team curry."

Monday night, 2230 hours

There was a definite cold snap to the air; it could be felt as soon as the sun set and grew stronger as the night wore on. The three doormen stamped their feet and clapped their gloved hands together as they stood outside the wine bar, opening and closing the doors for the patrons. They chatted and joked with each other and huddled in their long black coats against the frost and nodded heads in time with the base beat that pounded from inside.

Music filtered out onto the High Street each time the door was open and was muffled quickly again. The party was in full swing. The dance floor was crowded with young girls wearing next to nothing in the way only the young in winter can. The centre of attention was a small girl with black hair wearing pink and sporting a cheap plastic crown with "21 today!" on it. She had been drinking since the early afternoon, eager to start the party early, and was jumping enthusiastically around the dance floor.

Her friends squealed and giggled along with her, and the bouncers on the inside of the bar kept a close eye on the festivities. Anyone overeager or who thought dancing on the tables was a good idea was quickly dissuaded, and if they wanted to argue, they were escorted swiftly off the premises.

The licence holder was more than used to fights and police at his door and knew that he was walking a very fine line where the local licencing officer was concerned. He knew if he had one more incident involving police, his licence would be revoked and he would be out of business. The doormen had helped enormously, and there had been very little trouble since he had employed them.

He served behind the bar tonight, glad for the late licence he had been granted. This birthday party was going to make him a lot of money, even with the amount of soft drinks he was serving. He nodded to a regular who was lifting his empty beer glass from the end of the bar and made his way around his staff to re-fill it.

Matthew Westmore thanked the manager as he paid for his new pint and let his eyes scan the crowd. The music pounded through him like an incredible force, lifting his spirits and making him feel more alive. He wanted to dance, to move, and to run. Life was good for him at the moment; everything was going right for him for a change, and he felt incredible. The power rolled through him, and he wanted everyone to know it, to see it.

He breathed deeply and took in the scent of everyone in the bar. It was intoxicating, even more so than the beer in his hand. He could feel the youth, smell the sweat coming from the bodies of all these young, vibrant females. He wanted them all for himself.

Matthew downed his pint and then moved to the dance floor and the throng of people. He squeezed through the tightly packed mass, getting a high from the variety of smells.

He drew closer to the birthday girl and started to dance with her, pressing his body against hers and moving with the rhythm of the music, letting it take him over.

The friends of the birthday girl giggled awkwardly as she pushed Matthew away. He might be good looking, but she did not want some creepy stranger coming up to her and groping her.

Matthew grabbed her arm and pulled her towards him. She let out a scream and tried to pull away, yelling at her friends to get him off her. Her boyfriend, who had been at the bar getting in another round of drinks, moved in to help her.

Matthew could feel the angry energy coming from the young lad and smiled. As he felt the boyfriend grab him from behind, Matthew spun quickly to face him. With one arm, he lifted the boyfriend into the air and threw him towards the bar. The young lad was flying for a few seconds; then he crashed heavily into the bottles and shelves behind the bar.

Everything in the bar stopped save the music, and then the screaming began. The head bouncer and two doormen pounced on Matthew as the dance floor cleared. People ran for the exits, shouting and screaming in terror, tripping over each other and falling to the floor, which was soaked with booze and blood.

Matthew grinned as he took on the doormen. They were easy prey for him. One grabbed him from behind; the others grabbed an arm each. Matthew jerked his right arm, and the first doorman went flying towards the DJ, landing heavily on tables and chairs. Matthew grabbed the arm of the second and ripped. Screams punctuated the air as the second doorman had his arm ripped from the socket. That left the head doorman. He was a huge man, about a foot and a half taller than Matthew, but the latter lifted him in his powerful arms with ease. He hefted the man above his head, turned slowly, and with a growl, he let fly.

The head doorman sailed through the air, smashed through the glass of the window, and landed on the pavement outside, crushing some of the fleeing patrons.

Matthew launched himself through the broken window and landed softly on the pavement beside the head doorman. He looked around at the chaos he had caused, let out a growl, and ran off down the side street.

CHAPTER NINE

Monday night, 2330 hours

Inspector Kent surveyed the scene before her, her blue eyes intense and wary. One ambulance had just left for the hospital carrying the head doorman, who had a suspected broken back and numerous cuts from his collision with the window and the pavement. Another ambulance was tending to the youth who had thankfully stopped bleeding, and in the third, the paramedics were trying to calm down the doorman who had had his arm ripped out of its socket.

From this ambulance the voice of the section sergeant could be heard shouting, "Calm down! We're trying to help you!"

In a few moments they would be leaving for the hospital too, which just left another crime scene to cordon.

It had been utter chaos when Pete had first arrived on scene. People were running frantically to get away from the flying glass and the wounded, not to mention the flying bodies. Pete had called for assistance immediately using the emergency button on his radio; then he had attempted to make sense of the mess in front of him. A few members of the public had stayed and managed to give them descriptions of the suspect. All of them had positively identified Matthew Westmore as the suspect; some knew him personally.

Inspector Kent looked at the huge shattered window and shook her head in disbelief, wondering how a used-up druggie who was about a foot shorter than the smallest doorman had managed to toss the largest of them through the window as though he weighed nothing at all.

The owner of the bar was talking to night duty CID, and he was pale with shock. He kept asking after the lad that had been thrown over the bar. This was not going to do his business any good at all. The CID officer then walked over to the inspector.

"Guv, the owner of the bar gave us an address for Westmore," he said.

She nodded. "Right. Go back to the station, Steve, and check the address on the systems. See if it's known to us. Then we can let TSG and the firearms unit argue over who gives him an early wake-up call."

The CID officer nodded and went over to the unmarked car parked next to her marked supervisor's vehicle. Inspector Kent watched him leave and then went over to Pete.

"I've asked for some more bodies to help with the cordon," she told them. "CID just dealt with a call to the Quality Food Store. Apparently, Matthew's girlfriend Amy Farringdon went psycho and trashed the store." She shook her head. "What on earth is going on?"

"Well, it is nearly a full moon, guv," Pete said and then rolled his eyes as a television news van pulled up. He stared at the inspector.

"Sometimes, I hate being the boss," she muttered.

At that moment, the area car pulled up, and Lauren and Brett got out followed by a new person. He was tall and thin with short grey hair. Inspector Kent smiled as the man approached her and shook her hand.

"Chief Superintendent May," she greeted him.

"Kathy," he replied and then glanced over to the news van and the reporters straining over the police line. "So what can I tell them?"

"Go away?" she suggested with a glint in her eye.

He smiled grimly. "You know I would love to, but ..."

Inspector Kent nodded. "We have a named suspect. CID are doing some checks on a possible location. Then hopefully we can detain him."

Chief Superintendent May did not bother to hide the surprised expression on his face. "One suspect did all this?"

"Matthew Westmore has been identified by all the witnesses who did not run away from him, sir," Pete said.

May looked at him. "Is Westmore a possible for the murders as well?"

"Not that we know of, but he could be a factor," Inspector Kent told him.

Chief Superintendent May frowned. "It wasn't mentioned by the murder team this afternoon at the briefing."

"They did not know then, sir," she said, looking at Lauren. "PC Wylie thinks that a mental health disorder Westmore suffers from could be a possible motive for the murders. Whether he is working alone is another thing."

"OK. Even if it's only a possibility, I want him questioned. I want this over with, and TSG and firearms can do whatever they need to." He looked over at the news van. "Wish me luck with the wolves!" he said and then walked over to the cordon line.

Pete looked at Lauren. She seemed to be lost in thought. "What's up?"

She looked at him and smiled. "I was just thinking how my dad was his puppy walker when he first came out of Hendon."

Pete sniggered and took a deep breath. He found he was looking at the third ambulance as it pulled away. The doorman inside was as big as he was. It worried him that Westmore had shown such insane strength. He had known the drug addict for years and even had seen what he was capable of when he had taken drugs, but this was different. He was not the only person worried about the strength the man was supposed to have shown. The rest of the team wanted this set of nights to be over, and they wanted Westmore caught.

Monday night, 2345 hours

Kellie sat in the darkened control room and drummed her fingers on the desktop in front of her. She was on the support channel this evening and was sitting at the terminal next to the controller. She had three small flat computer screens in front of her; one was the main control-room screen where the next call popped up on the list, the second was the controls for the CCTV of the station, and the third was a working system screen where she could check any reports for officers.

She stared at the blue screen of the call terminal, where the yellow text of the call, highlighted by a red box, described what had happened at the bar. There had been something playing on her mind since the briefing, and it was beginning to annoy her.

Kellie looked at her controller, Mike, who was busy supervising every call that popped up on the screen. "Mike, have you got the daily briefing pack with the names of the murder victims on it?" she asked.

Mike looked behind him and reached for a blue folder on the bookcase. He handed it to her. "What's up?"

She shrugged as she looked through the folder. "I don't know. When I was front office, Matthew used to come in all the time, high as a kite, making allegations. I just want to check something."

Kellie logged on to the intelligence system and typed in several names. A number of hits came up, and she read through every report.

"I knew it!" she exclaimed.

"What?" Mike asked.

"I've found some links between Matthew and our victims from a report I put on three years ago." She slammed the slow mouse on the desk, cursed it, and then printed off several reports.

"Well done, love," Mike said.

"Can I leave for a minute to take this next door to the DI?" she asked.

Mike nodded. Kellie unplugged her headset and walked over to the printer to retrieve the reports. She left the control room and walked next door to the writing room, which was also the briefing room.

Uniformed officers she did not know milled around – TSG and SO19 waiting for the rest to arrive and the briefing to start. A white board had been brought in, and the DI from the murder squad stood before this with the inspectors from TSG and SO19.

Kellie approached him nervously. "Sir, can I have a word, please?"

DI Sprite looked up from the paperwork he and the other inspectors were going through and smiled at Kellie. "Yeah, sure, love. How can I help?"

She stood next to him and handed him the reports she had printed. "Sir, I used to be a station officer, and I had a lot of dealings with Matthew and his mates," she explained. "He was in all the time, because whenever he got his benefit he either lost it or it was robbed."

DI Sprite grinned. "Station office hasn't changed since my day then," he said. He read through the report, and his eyes went wide. "Hang on! This report says he was robbed by our gang of victims, minus the little lad."

Kellie nodded. "They were always turning him over, but he could never give us their names, as he was so spaced. As you can see, I put their names down because I overheard them bragging about how many times they had robbed him when they were in front office signing on for bail. Wasted Westmore, they used to call him." The DI handed the reports to the other inspectors, but Kellie hadn't finished. "So when I looked at everything to do

Claws and Robbers

with Matthew and the first victim, it turns out that he got Matthew hooked on drugs. He used to sell to him."

"Bloody hell! Are you sure?"

"It's all there, sir. Matthew was sold drugs by the first victim and robbed by the others, except Jack, who hadn't joined the gang then," Kellie said.

DI Sprite waved the papers around. "This is incredible, officer," he said, a huge smile on his face. Kellie beamed as he put an arm around her shoulders and turned to the officers in the room. "This is why civilians are the backbone of the Met. Well done, love. What would we do without you?"

"Well, er, you would have to do my job," Kellie remarked.

DI Sprite let out a laugh and then moved back to the front of the room. "Right then, you lot. It looks like Matthew Westmore definitely is a suspect for the murders too."

Tuesday morning, 0500 hours

At the junction of the quiet residential street the van was parked, ready to transport the prisoner to custody. Pete let out a yawn and watched as TSG and the firearms units discussed who was going in first. There was radio silence until the operation was over, and everything had been discussed at the station before they left.

SO19 Gold, the call sign for the firearms inspector, stood next to the inspector for TSG, call sign Silver, and they debated about the best approach. The target house was halfway along the residential street, and as the more respectable neighbours would be setting off for work soon, they did not have a lot of time to spare.

Pete looked at the street and then glanced at Andrew. "I don't know how Westmore managed to get a place here. It's a nice road – or was," he commented.

"How long has he been active on the division?" Andrew asked.

"Oh, about seven years altogether. He was always in custody, and the courts would always release him. He was then finally put away but, as you heard, was released yet again. I haven't seen him for about two years, but once seen, never forgotten."

THE SO19 Inspector walked over to the van. "Can we borrow your probationer?" he asked.

Andrew paled.

"What for, guv?"

"We've decided the best move is to send in the TSG, but we need an officer to knock on the door for us."

"Isn't the suspect armed, sir?" Pete asked.

"No guns were mentioned. We're going to stay outside and cover with baton guns, ready to go in if he has any knives, but from your own reports, this guy is not armed."

Andrew slid out of the van and walked around to meet the inspector, glad he was wearing his Met vest.

The SO19 inspector went through with Andrew what he wanted him to do, and after being briefed, all the officers took their positions.

The TSG went round the back to cover any escape route, and the rest walked behind Andrew, one of them carrying the bright red enforcer and all of them wearing full riot gear. SO19 took up position to cover. Four followed the TSG and hid behind the garden hedge on the pavement.

Andrew took a deep breath and walked up the garden path on his own. The porch door was brand new and gleaming white. He jumped as the next-door neighbour opened his front door and was pushed back inside by the firearms officers.

He knocked on the door. There was no reply. He glanced over his shoulder at the TSG sergeant, who gave a signal. The TSG officer with the enforcer stepped up. With a swing he hit the lock, and with a loud crack, the door opened. He took the second door easily and then stood aside to let his colleagues rush in.

They yelled, kicking open doors and storming into each room. Andrew gaped as he saw the suspect at the top of the flight of stairs. The three TSG officers came in from the back, and the others ran up the stairs to get Westmore.

Matthew slipped his legs over the banister smoothly and dropped softly to the floor, as lithe as a cat. His eyes darted to the officers around him as they turned to come back after him. He pounced up and made a run for the front door. Andrew stood in the doorway and was knocked flying. The young officer was aware of people behind him, but instinct told him to grip Westmore's legs. For a few moments he felt himself being thrown about as if on a roller coaster at the fairground, and he felt sick. Then there was a press of bodies as SO19 and TSG piled on top of them, screaming for Westmore to lie still.

Matthew stopped struggling under the sheer weight and held his arms wide to show he was harmless.

The officers got off him. He was handcuffed and brought to his feet. Matthew looked at all the officers around him then fixed his stare on Andrew. Andrew shivered and could not hold the stare.

The only other person in the house was a tall skinny male with long, dark brown hair, and he was brought out of the house by two officers. He was begging to be released. One TSG officer cuffed him and held him up against the front garden hedge.

"We need another van on the scene. We have one further detainee," called the officer on his radio.

"Please! You must let me go!" the man cried.

Matthew was put into the back of the van, and Andrew got into the front once more. Pete looked over his shoulder at the suspect, and at first he did not recognise him.

"Hello, Matthew. You're looking a lot better. You off the drugs?" he asked.

Matthew squinted at him through the enforced cage at the rear of the van. "I can smell the fear on your little puppy," he growled.

Pete nodded. "Now be nice, or you won't get your cup of tea at the station."

Pete pulled the van away from the scene.

"What's your name?" the TSG officer asked.

"Daniel!" said the man.

"Do you have anything sharp in your pockets or anything which may harm me, Daniel?"

He shook his head and then cried out in pain.

"What's wrong, Daniel? Do you need an ambulance?"

He shook his head. "Let me go!" he said, his voice tight with strain. Again the man cried out in pain.

The TSG officer tried to grab his forearm to stop him struggling against the handcuffs at his back. One of his colleagues moved over to help after helping to put Matthew in the van.

The man began to jerk his arms in the cuffs hard, drawing blood. He yelled again to be set free.

"Please, let me go! I can't control it!" he panted.

The two TSG officers exchanged a glance and grabbed an arm each. They then tried to place him on the ground in an attempt to control him. The man threw his head back and yelled, and more officers came to assist. Then the man began to growl. The TSG officers holding his arms felt his muscles rip and convulse, and they yelled at him to calm down. Again he growled and then turned it to a howl which sent chills down the spines of the officers present.

The shirt the man was wearing began to rip at the sleeves, and the TSG officers came into contact with his flesh. It was burning hot to the touch, and these had to be the hairiest arms they had felt. Both were knocked to the ground as the man pushed them away. He spun to face them and hissed at them, showing teeth that were unbelievably sharp, almost like fangs.

The man then seemed to grow before their eyes. There was a wrenching and then a popping sound, and a set of static handcuffs fell to the ground.

The man ran off down the street, and a few officers gave chase, but they lost him. One of the TSG officers put an urgent call in to the control room, and one of the carriers gave chase, blue lights flashing.

The SO19 officer lowered his baton gun and exchanged a look of terror with his colleagues. "What the fuck was that?"

CHAPTER TEN

Tuesday morning, 1000 hours

Jack opened the door that led out to the front office of the police station. The main waiting area was full, and there was already a queue of people to the front door waiting for the solitary station officer to get to them. Jack was careful to not make eye contact as the crowd seemed to shuffle as one and look at him in the hope that he was there to serve them. It was a standard duck-and-run method he had picked up when not working in the front office. It was not good to be chased by a member of public who wanted to speak to an officer straight away because of the dog poo on his pavement. Failure to drop everything to deal with the matter was met with demands about what they did do for all that money the tax payer gave them.

Jack walked over to the elderly gentleman on the bench reading a thick book. He wore a pinstripe suit and small metal-rimmed glasses. A large briefcase sat by his feet.

"Mr Baker?" Jack asked.

The solicitor looked up and smiled, a look of surprise on his face. "Goodness, that was quick," he said. "Usually it takes a while for someone to come and get me."

Jack nodded. "Well, we're ready to go, sir."

"After I consult with my client, of course," the solicitor said.

The solicitor stood up, shook hands with Jack, and followed him through to the custody suite. One of the custody sergeants looked up from his desk and began the procedure of signing the solicitor in.

Jack went through a side door and behind the two sergeants, where several clipboards leaned against a wall, one for each cell with a constantly updated record of each prisoner. He lifted the one for Matthew Westmore down and brought it out for the solicitor to go through.

The small man leafed through each page of the record and appeared to nod slightly. "I would like a copy please," he requested.

The sergeant nodded and printed another record off from the computer while the jailer went to get Matthew.

Matthew had been placed in a camera cell, and his movements were constantly monitored by the jailer, who also made half-hourly checks on him. At that moment, Matthew was lying on the bench that served as a bed. He looked relaxed and had his hands clasped behind his head, and his ice-blue eyes stared at the camera. He was wearing a white forensic suit after having his own clothes seized for examination.

Matthew walked softly along the corridor, watching the officers as he passed them by. Jack was reminded of the man he had met at the mansion, almost stalking as opposed to walking. Matthew looked at Jack as he approached and met his grey eyes.

Jack felt shivers run down his spine and pulled himself taller. He was head and shoulders above Matthew in height but did not make the error of assuming he was the stronger.

There was an air about Matthew, something in the way he held himself, which was superior. He smiled pleasantly at the solicitor and then nodded politely to Jack.

The jailer escorted them into one of the three interview rooms.

Jack seemed to visibly shrink as he let out a breath. "Arrogant little arse!" he muttered.

"You do know there is full audio and visual recording in this custody suite," the custody sergeant reminded him with a wry smile on his face.

Jack looked at him. "Yeah, and I know that this is our man. He may not have done this alone, but he is our man." He sighed and shook his head. "Well, I'll be in CID when they are finished with the consultation."

Claws and Robbers

DI Sprite stood in front of the white board at the front of the conference room. On the board behind him was the new custody photograph of Matthew Westmore together with photos of his known associates, which included his girlfriend, Amy Farringdon. Night duty CID had left the report reference and the stills from the CCTV of the damage she had done in the shop, along with the statement from the store owner that she had boasted about being the blonde suspect from the first murder. None of Matthew's friends had been at the house they found him in except for the one who had escaped, but neighbours had seen them all there.

On a table was a wooden evidence box containing the pair of quick cuffs shattered during Daniel's escape. Officers kept going over the box to look at it and marvel how anyone could have shattered them with strength alone. Jack sat at the front off to one side, watching what was happening.

"Right, it was brought to our attention that Westmore is suffering from a psychological disorder. We found Triazapan and Diazapan, which supports this theory, plus he knew all the victims. The first was his dealer; the rest apparently robbed him a lot. The doctor has been to see him and states he is fit for interview. The duty solicitor has arrived and is in consultation with him at the moment."

Ted walked into the office, an unhappy expression wrinkling his face. "SOCO just got the lab return back from the blood found at the first scene," he said.

"I take it the news is not good from the look on your face," Jack said.

"The sample was contaminated. In the foreign DNA taken from the first victim there was a human sample, but it was so mixed up with canine DNA that there is no chance of identifying it."

"Shit!" Jack cursed. "What do we do now?"

"Maybe we can go back to our fighting dogs theory?" the DI suggested. "Can we speak to Vicky Harper again and maybe ask her about the canine DNA?"

Jack shook his head. "No, we focus on Matthew, boss. He is involved with this; I'd bet money on it." He looked down at his A4 notebook, where he had jotted down his notes and a list of questions for his interview plan. It also held a computer disc. "We have the CCTV from the bar showing him ripping the arm off a bouncer who was twice his size. That was some insane strength there, and if he was high enough, he could have ripped the other victims apart."

"But without the forensic or physical evidence, we've got nothing," the

DI said. "Unless we can explain how that DNA became contaminated, there is nothing forensically linking Westmore to either murder scene."

Tuesday afternoon, 1400 hours

The soundproofed interview room was small; it had a desk positioned along one wall with two chairs to either side of it. A flat-screen television hung on the wall, and on the desk was a DVD player and a cassette recorder. The walls and the carpet were dark blue, and there were no windows to the outside world. A panic strip ran along each wall, and the light above the door shone red, indicating that it was occupied.

Interview rooms usually made Jack feel comfortable; with his plan in his notebook, he could guide and control the conversation and get the result he wanted. Suspects were usually uneasy in the small, windowless room and did not want to spend any more time in there than was absolutely necessary, but this was different. Jack felt oppressed in that room and longed for an excuse to end the interview, but he had to keep going.

It had been two hours of Jack asking the same questions over and over with the same response: "No comment." Jack was annoyed and frustrated, and all he wanted to do was smack Matthew around his smug little face, but he controlled himself. This was why he wrote down his list of questions – as frustrating as no-comment interviews were, as the officer leading it, he had to keep asking the questions.

Andrea squirmed in the seat next to him, as annoyed as he was. The solicitor sat next to Matthew and wrote notes in his own book, looking at his client every so often with a very strange, smug expression on his face.

Jack decided to resort to the CCTV footage. Neither Matthew nor his solicitor had seen it yet, but they had been told about it. The DI was talking with the Crown Prosecution Service about the charges they could bring against Matthew as a result of the film.

He played it for them, and Matthew stared at himself on the screen, and Jack could have sworn he was enjoying it a little too much. Jack pressed the pause button on the remote, halted the film and looked at Matthew again.

"I understand you were once a drug addict, Matthew," he said. No reply. "Addiction is such a horrible disease, isn't it? You lose all control over your life, and you become weak, vulnerable to manipulation by others." No answer.

"The first victim, Jake McDonald, used to be your dealer, Matthew. He got you hooked on drugs. He made you weak."

"No comment."

"It's all in previous reports, Matthew. It is all fact. Just like those kids who used to rob you all the time."

"No comment."

Jack grinned. "Every time you got your benefit, they would be waiting for you outside the post office, and those little gits would take your money, wouldn't they?"

"No comment."

"No comment? You have made several crime reports about them." He waved some sheets of paper. "I have all the report reference numbers here, Matthew. You have direct links to all of our victims."

"No comment."

Jack sat forward, leaning his arms on the desk. "Coming out of your addiction must have been like waking up after a nightmare. Realising what they had done to you must have made you feel very angry." He shrugged. "It would have made me angry, Matthew."

Matthew's blue eyes stared at the screen, seemingly oblivious to Jack's words.

Jack looked back at the screen. "I have never, in all my years in this job, seen strength like yours, Matthew." He looked down at his own palms. "The power you have in your hands. If I had that kind of strength and a bunch of snotty little punks had robbed me, I would want to make them pay." Jack nodded. "I understand, Matthew. Is that what happened – you wanted to make them pay and you lost control?"

Jack waited again for a response, but Matthew continued to look at the screen.

"Are you not even going to tell me what your secret is? You went from being a drug addict close to death to a man so strong he ripped a bouncer's arm off. That man was twice your size! You're clean, you're healthy, and you are very strong. How did you do it?"

Slowly, Matthew moved his blue eyes and stared deeply into Jack's. "No comment," he said softly.

The two custody sergeants leaned back in their chairs and laughed. DI Sprite stood behind the custody desk, leaning against the waist-high bookcases that sat along the wall. He sipped a cup of tea as he related the story from his beat days.

"So me and the boys are stood there in this shed with this naked bloke who has a nappy on. We're trying to talk to him whilst he's screaming about his zombie girlfriend, and he's got this garden trowel as a weapon. Then the nappy falls off, and we can then see where his key ring has gone!"

They all laughed again, and one of the sergeants wiped the tears from his eyes. "Reminds me of when—"

He broke off as the door to interview room 1 opened and Jack came out, followed by Andrea, Matthew, and the solicitor.

DI Sprite looked at Jack and could see the interview had not gone well. Jack approached the custody desk carrying the paperwork and tapes. He booked Matthew back into the cell, and the jailer escorted him down.

The solicitor seemed to relax a little, and Jack looked relieved to be away from the prisoner.

"Can I get my client something to eat, sergeant?" he asked as he signed the paperwork.

The sergeant looked to DI Sprite, who nodded. "No problem with that, sir," he said.

Once done, the solicitor was escorted out by Andrea. DI Sprite frowned at Jack, who had not said anything since leaving the room.

"Excuse us, fellas," DI Sprite said.

He moved around the desk to Jack and escorted him from the custody suite. Jack walked as fast as he could, and the DI found it a struggle to keep up. He strode out to the yard and headed for the smoking area by the dog kennels and stopped, leaning against the wall and ran his fingers through his hair.

"You look like you've seen a ghost," DI Sprite said.

Jack looked towards the police building and the custody suite. "Not here. He can hear us," Jack whispered.

DI Sprite screwed his face up. "What do you mean?"

Jack sighed and continued to stare at custody.

DI Sprite had worked with Jack for years and had never seen him like this.

"Come on, let's get out of here."

DI Sprite put the small glass of whiskey in front of Jack and sat opposite him with his lemonade. "Drink that," he instructed.

Jack turned his nose up at the drink. "I don't like whiskey, boss," he said.

"Don't care – you need it. That's an order," he said.

Jack reluctantly picked up the glass and began to sip, making a face as he did so. The DI laughed at him and then became serious.

"So why are you so freaked?" he asked.

Jack shook his head. "I don't know, boss. That guy scared the hell out of me."

"That little pipsqueak? How could he scare you?"

"I don't know. He was 'no comment' all the way through, but when he looked at me, I could feel him thinking about how he was going to kill me."

"You're serious, aren't you?"

Jack nodded.

"Jesus! Did he say anything about the murders at all?"

"No, just loved watching himself tear those bouncers apart like it was a porn movie. His only answer was 'no comment' throughout, even after I linked him to the victims. He did it, boss. After that interview I am sure, but he didn't admit anything."

The DI drank his lemonade. "Take the night off Jack," he said. "CPS are willing to charge him for GBH times three, affray, and aggravated assault, and we have an extension to interview him again tomorrow. I'll have a go at the little shit."

Jack smiled. "Now you versus him I would like to see, boss."

CHAPTER ELEVEN

Tuesday night, 2027 hours

Inspector Kent walked into the ladies' toilet and went over to the mirrors. She ran her fingers through her collar-length light brown hair and straightened her shirt. A frown creased her brow as she heard someone crying quietly in one of the cubicles.

She looked over her shoulder towards the closed cubicle door and walked over to it. Lightly she tapped on the door and pressed her ear against it. "Hello?" she called softly.

The crying stopped abruptly, and a moment later the toilet flushed. Inspector Kent stepped back as the door opened and Lauren emerged.

"Lauren? What's wrong?" she asked, taking in her red and puffy eyes.

Lauren went over to one of the sinks, filled it with water, and began to splash her face and eyes. "Sorry, guv. I'll be fine for parade," she said, her voice hoarse.

Inspector Kent stood beside her. "Not bothered about parade, Lauren. I've never seen you like this. What's wrong?"

"Something I should not bring in to work, boss."

"I don't want you to tell me because of some job welfare crap. You look as though you need to talk to someone."

Lauren sniffed miserably and looked up at the older woman, her eyes brimming with concern. "Just a spot of man trouble. I'll be fine. Promise."

Inspector Kent glanced at her watch. "I could use a cigarette," she said. "Grab some tissues, and we'll chat out in the yard."

Lauren let out a sigh. She was torn between embarrassment and shame, and she did not want to admit it or tell anyone about it, but then she nodded and grabbed a wad of tissues from one of the cubicles. She followed the inspector down the two stories and out into the back yard. The inspector commented for what had to be the hundredth time about the Met male chauvinists not designing a police building with a ladies' toilet on every floor like the men had.

Lauren smiled wanly and felt very glad that they did not see anyone else on the stairs down. It was bad enough that her inspector had discovered her crying. If she had seen anyone she knew and they had asked after her, she was afraid that she might have started crying again. That was one of the good things about nights and handover period.

Inspector Kent walked across the yard towards the dog kennels and leaned against the wall and lit a cigarette. She took a drag and then fixed Lauren with her pale blue eyes.

"So what kind of man trouble has got you so upset that you're crying in a toilet?"

Lauren blew her nose. It sounded so pathetic, put like that. And she felt pathetic, allowing something so small get to her. She looked up at the cloudy sky. "I've been dumped," she replied glumly. She sighed again. "It all sounds so stupid. I'm old enough to deal better with this. I mean, it wasn't as though we were serious."

"Still, no one likes to be dumped. Was this your mystery man everyone was talking about?"

Lauren wanted the ground to swallow her. She rolled her eyes and took a deep breath. "I thought only a few people knew I was seeing someone."

Kent smirked. "This is the Met. Nothing is secret. Why all the secrecy anyway?"

Lauren shrugged her shoulders. "He wanted it that way. Said he didn't want to go public until he was absolutely sure of his feelings."

"Why?"

"He told me he had a really bad history with his ex. She really messed with his head, and he was just getting over a breakdown because of what she did." She felt a spark of anger. "Turns out he has gone back to his ex-girlfriend."

The inspector took another drag of her cigarette. "When did he end it?"

Lauren looked at her briefly. "He called me on the phone last night, just after parade."

Inspector Kent looked stunned and disgusted at the same time. "He dumped you over the phone?" she asked, incredulous. She shifted position slightly to face her. "Is he job?"

Lauren nodded. "I was getting pissed off with him anyway. Every time he treated me like dirt and I objected, he always threw her treatment of him back in my face. I shouldn't be made to feel guilty about telling him off for treating me like crap. You know me, guv – I don't take bullshit in any relationship, and if I don't like something, I say it. He made me feel bad for speaking up."

"Would you mind telling me who he is?"

Something in the inspector's voice made Lauren look at her. The expression on the older woman's face was expectant, almost as if she knew who it was already.

"Kenny Robbins, a PC on B team," she said quietly, feeling sick and grief stricken all over again at uttering his name out loud.

The inspector let out a sigh and hung her head for a moment. "I might have known," she said.

Lauren pushed aside her pain, intrigued by her reaction. The inspector looked at her again.

"He has been lying to you, Lauren. His inspector was telling me about a drink up they had last week, celebrating his engagement."

Lauren felt the anger rise in her. "What!" she exclaimed. "He was still seeing me then!"

"He's an arsehole, Lauren. I was his skipper at Battersea a few years ago, and I never liked him. Even then I thought he was a sleaze – a micro-cop who thought he knew it all just out the doors of Hendon. He became involved with a female PC on another team. He really messed with her head, and he fed her the exact same lies he told you. And all the while he was still with his girlfriend."

Lauren's eyes widened with fury. "He knew I would never touch him whilst he was with someone else. I would not do that to myself or another woman. Bastard!"

"As I said, he's done it before, to a very good friend of mine." Kent smiled. "He wanted to come to our team when he first arrived on borough, but I refused to have him. I do not want him anywhere near my officers. He's a shit officer but never seems to do anything bad enough for us to get rid of him."

Lauren shook her head. "What a dick! He lied to me about everything!"

Part of her did not want to believe that Kenny was so nasty. She could not understand why he had lied to her about his girlfriend just to get into bed with her. It made her feel awful that she had essentially been party to his affair, and that she had been ignorant of that fact was irrelevant to her. She felt like such an idiot. She had never wanted to start a relationship and had only started seeing Kenny as a friend. Then, one day, he was telling her he had just got over a breakdown after his girlfriend dumped him but that he wanted to try again with her.

However, she had to remember that she had begun to see through him. The note he had left and his constant excuses about how his wrongs were because of his ex, who was probably a very nice woman, had made her rethink the hassle of being with him. If truth be told, part of her had known the relationship was wrong, and she had been planning to end it. So was she upset because he had done it first?

Lauren felt so stupid – that she had fallen for everything he had said, that he had managed to get past her instincts and defences so easily. "What shall I do, guv? I'm going to bump into him a lot here."

"Cut him off completely. Cold turkey, Lauren, pretend he is dead. I can even warn him off if you like." She grinned. "Strangely, most people on this Borough think he is a twat too. Once they find out what he did to you, he'll have no friends left. You are very popular, and most officers I speak to love working with you."

Lauren felt the tears sting her eyes. She was reminded of a seminar her dad sometimes gave, and in part of it he spoke about strange wake-up calls and how when things went from bad to worse, someone would say or do something and it would be a wake-up call. This was definitely one of those times. She still felt like crap, but the anger she felt was now beginning to overtake that. Kenny was not on duty that night, but if he had been, Lauren did not think she would have been able to control her rage.

"Go and get a coffee. I'll tell the team you're speaking to CID again, and I'll post you as my driver tonight. Then this Friday night I'll come over to yours and we'll have a wine and chocolate night."

Lauren smiled, and the inspector reached out and gave her a hug.

"And remember, if you ever start to believe there is anything wrong with you, he is the one that dumped you – over the phone whilst you were at work. The twat!"

Lauren nodded, and they walked towards the main building, the inspector keeping an arm around her waist. She felt drained suddenly but relieved too, and her dad had always said that was a good sign. Feeling a sense of disappointed defeat, she knew she needed to let Jack know that it would be just her for Sunday dinner.

The inspector gave her another hug, then let her go and went through the back door to get to the parade room. Lauren went through the cage that covered the access to custody. The cold anger burned inside her, and all she wanted to do was beat Kenny repeatedly. The sensation made her hands tingle with the anticipation of it.

She walked up the ramp inside the cage and through the door that led into the main custody suite. For a change, all was quiet. The civilian jailer from late turn was leaning by the grille door, indulging in a coffee and chatting to Matthew Westmore, who was sitting on the bench sipping a cup of tea.

Matthew met her gaze. "Evening, miss," he said.

Lauren could not hide her surprise at the change in Matthew. Pete had told her he looked different, but she was not prepared for so drastic a transformation.

"You're looking well, Matthew," she commented.

He gave her a lopsided grin. "As do you," he replied.

She walked into the night duty kitchen and made herself a tea. While it was brewing, she watched Matthew through the small window in the door.

There was no such thing as werewolves. Her dad had done a programme on how the myth had originated, and it was basically a paedophile that assaulted and butchered children in a remote German village in the fifteen hundreds. No one then could conceive of such an evil, and it being such a religiously steeped time, when the killer's daughter spoke about him becoming a monster, they took that literally.

Lycanthropy was a mental condition which quite often coincided with bipolar disorder or schizophrenia, and the medications prescribed to treat it were the same.

Matthew looked completely normal; Lauren looked for any signs that he was suffering from the disorder, but there were none. He must have seen the doctor for his medication, but lycanthropy would still show symptoms.

Sipping her tea, she walked out of the kitchen and over to the raised desk where one of the two custody sergeants sat.

Matthew was laughing about something with the jailer. Lauren looked at the paper on the desk; she skipped past the busty page three to the horoscope by the fanatical psychic.

"You're not into that crap, are you?" one of the sergeants asked.

"It's always good for a laugh, skip," she replied.

Her eyes scanned down the column to Aquarius and read the first line. "The full moon tonight spells dramatic changes to your work and love life."

She looked at Matthew. Night had fallen, the moon was out, and if he really had lycanthropy, he would have been climbing the walls by now.

Lauren frowned and turned to walk from custody. The jailer took the cup from Matthew and threw it in the bin. Matthew stood up and moved close to Lauren. He matched her in height, and their eyes met on the same level.

His blue eyes sparkled; he gave her a slightly dreamy smile and moved closer to her. "I'll see you later, miss."

Lauren felt herself jolt awake as though something which had been clouding her insides had cleared like a morning mist hit by the sun. She felt everything around her become astoundingly clear, sharp, and loud. Then the sensation was gone.

She walked from the custody suite and went back out into the yard to complete the checks on the inspector's car.

Tuesday night, 2200 hours

Marcus stood in the rear gardens of the mansion and gazed up at the full moon. It was a myth that werewolves were controlled by the phases of the moon, but he would have been lying if he had denied that he felt the power of it. The night was crisp, and a frost hung in the air that would cover the grounds in a white sheen in the morning. Tonight the air was ethereal and full of wonder, seeming to shimmer all around him.

The air was cold on his naked skin as he stood there with nine of his fellow alphas, their first betas accompanying him. The magnitude of this ceremony had quieted chatter, and there was a solemnity about this night that had everyone silently examining their own thoughts.

There had been fear earlier in the day when the main part of the meeting had taken place. The threat of exposure had everyone worried and no doubt would be the main topic of discussion for months to come. The others had agreed that Marcus as overall alpha should take the lead in matters. It was an honour with two edges: one guaranteed him autonomy over how media exposure, if any, was handled, and the other made sure that he would be the scapegoat if it all went wrong. He would be a very public face that, if it was not accepted, could be disposed of.

The European pack alpha had made it clear that if this went wrong, he would challenge Marcus directly for leadership. Jacques' vote of no confidence in Marcus had been crude and obvious, but that was another problem for another day.

Ingrid stepped in front of Marcus, her thickly gloved hands holding the silver gauntlet ready for him to put on. He smiled at his first and then looked down the two rows of men and women, all naked in the moonlight, and nodded.

Marcus took a deep breath and braced his body, ready. He jerked his head to the side and stretched his spine up as tall as it could go. He could feel the vertebrae popping, stretching, and reconnecting and could feel the muscles pulse and rip. He let out a growl that became louder and deeper, felt the sweat run off him, and howled with the pain as his body readjusted.

His eyes squinted at the intensity of the colours of the night-time world, and his elongated snout inhaled the new world. He looked at the alphas and saw the half wolf in all of them, panting and recovering from the Change that was never smooth and always hurt to some degree.

He flexed his clawed forearm and then slid it slowly into the gauntlet Ingrid held. The inside was soft velvet, and as an alpha he was more resistant to silver than the others. He held the gauntlet up as Ingrid stepped away and waited for the others to be ready. He then gave the signal for the prisoner to be brought out.

Robin was dumped in front of the gauntlet and shivered as the cold air hit his naked skin. Ingrid stood over him and waited. He looked at the two rows of alphas, who waited. There was no going back now.

Slowly, he got to his feet and shuffled towards the alphas. His heart thundered in his ears, and he trembled with fear and apprehension. If he survived this, in one month he could return, forgiven for what he had created.

He reached the first two. As he stepped in between them, they each struck with their silver gloves. He screamed in pain and felt the sting as his blood was exposed to the air.

He moved to the second pair, and they hit his back, one after the other, ripping bloody rents in his flesh. He gasped and cried as the silver scorched him and made him howl in agony. The third pair marked his chest, whipping their gauntlets through his skin as deep as they dared.

He fell to the cold grass, tears streaming down his face, his body inflamed from the reaction to the silver. They waited patiently. They were in no rush at all. He forced himself to his knees, got one foot under him and then the other. He staggered to the fourth pair, who scored more gashes along his ribs and back.

Robin gasped for breath and did not think he could take any more. Blood ran into his eyes from where someone had caught his forehead, and he could only make out a blur ahead. However, he knew that Mike and his own alpha were next. Mike, in half-wolf form with beautiful ebony fur, glared at Robin with green eyes. He held aloft his gauntlet and brought it down on Robin's chest, making a hideous pattern of furrows in his flesh.

Last was Marcus. His beautiful, pale brown fur shimmered in the moonlight, and his violet eyes glowed. He stood tall and commanding, and the energy rolling from him radiated a calmness that must be obeyed. Robin looked up at him, feeling adoration for his leader and wretched for having betrayed him.

Marcus took his gauntlet and gently touched the tips of the claws to Robin's throat. He pressed, and Robin howled as the silver bit into his neck. Ever so slowly, Marcus dragged the gauntlet across Robin's neck and down his chest.

Marcus stepped into Robin's space, his snout touching the tip of his nose. He then stabbed Robin in the gut with the gauntlet. Robin gasped and collapsed against his alpha. The claws were then ripped out and across, spraying blood in the air, and the prisoner was cast onto the ground.

Marcus stepped back and looked down at the poor unfortunate soul at his feet; he then pointedly turned his back on the traitor. The other alphas followed suit.

Ingrid squatted down beside Robin and checked that he was still alive. He would heal – no doubt about that – but it would take longer because of the reaction to the silver. She looked up at James.

"Take this little cock and dump him outside the civvie hospital. For one month he is dead to the pack."

CHAPTER TWELVE

Wednesday morning, 0200 hours

Andrew walked behind the custody desk and sat down in the chair next to the sergeant. He took down the clipboards from the wall behind him, checked the time on the digital wall clock, and put an entry on each custody record.

The sergeant pressed a button on his laptop computer and resumed the movie they had been watching. All was quiet in custody that night, and the other sergeant had taken a walk around the yard to get some fresh air.

Andrew took another bite of his sandwich and contemplated looking over his textbooks for one of the probationer exams he would have to take in the next few weeks.

Matthew Westmore leapt up from his bed and began to pace his cell impatiently. Andrew watched on one of the monitors situated on the desk in front of him. He stood up, keeping a careful eye as the pacing became more anxious, and then started slightly as Matthew began to pound on the cell door.

"Let me out!" he screamed.

"Shit!" said the sergeant. "Go and see what he wants."

Andrew sighed and walked back up to the cells, the custody keys jingling on his belt. He checked the peephole and then pulled down the door wicket and looked at a distraught Matthew.

"You have to let me out of here!" he gasped.

"What's the problem, Matthew?" he asked.

Even as he asked the question, Andrew knew Matthew was not right. Since he had been brought in, he had been calm and quiet, but now he stared at Andrew in terror, his face had gone bright red, and the sweat was pouring off him.

"Sarge!" Andrew shouted. "I think we need an ambulance!"

The sergeant looked at the monitor as Matthew began to pound on the walls as though he were trying to break through them. A loud cry erupted from his body and turned into a spine-chilling scream.

Matthew ripped the clothes from his body, the heat boiling inside him. The sergeant pressed the panic alarm and got on the phone to the control room and yelled for an ambulance and assistance. He jumped over the raised counter and ran down to the cells as Andrew slammed the wicket shut and grabbed for the keys attached to his belt.

Matthew screamed again, the noise waking up the other prisoners. A ripping noise could be heard through the door followed by the sickening sound of bones popping and cracking.

The sergeant hit the panic strip again even though he could hear the buzz of it echoing through the suite, and a cold sweat broke out over his body. He did not want to be the sergeant on duty with a death in custody.

Andrew put the key in the lock as Pete and Darren ran into custody.

Andrew paused as the noise in the cell suddenly stopped. The sounds of the other prisoners seemed muffled as the officers strained to hear what was going on in Matthew's cell.

There was a low rumbling from within. Andrew and the sergeant exchanged a look. Andrew's hand reached out cautiously to turn the key.

The cell door buckled outward as it was hit from the other side. Andrew dove out of the way, and the sergeant jumped back. They stared open-mouthed.

Claws ripped through the reinforced metal of the door as though it were made of paper. Pete withdrew his asp and flicked it open as the door was punched out into the corridor in a heap of twisted metal. Concrete and plaster from the walls blew out in chunks, and dust clouded the air.

Pete's jaw dropped as a creature stepped out and stared directly at him.

The thing stood over six feet tall; had a broad, muscular chest; and was covered head to toe with pale blonde fur. It had large, powerful arms and hands that ended in lethal-looking claws. Pete looked up at the face, already registering the fact that this thing was indeed male, and then checked his sanity. What he was looking at was impossible. It could not be real – the large head with the long snout, the vicious white fangs, the pointed ears, and the blue eyes. Pete knew he was looking at Matthew and that Matthew was looking back at him. Pete saw it and could not believe it.

He pressed the emergency button on his radio. "Urgent assistance required in custody!" he cried, raising his asp.

A dart flew through the air and struck Matthew on his right arm. Darren covered his ears as the howl of pain screeched through the custody suite, echoing off the walls. The creature pulled the six-inch dart from his arm and let it drop to the floor, where his blood sizzled in reaction to it.

He ducked as another dart flew and missed. His lips curled back in a snarl as he looked beyond the officers.

Liv ran full pelt towards the wolf, screaming at her teammates to get out of the way. For a split second they stood there motionless. Then, seeming to comprehend on instinct that she knew what she was doing, they moved.

The creature moved to attack, clawed hands ready to strike. Liv slipped to the floor and pulled her silver dagger. She slid easily along the polished concrete and vinyl floor and struck out at his leg, trying to hamstring him.

Another howl echoed, and the creature bolted. He launched himself past the officers into the main booking area. Liv sprang to her feet and gave chase.

"Shit!" she cursed, pulling another dart and holding it in her free hand.

She shouted for the officers to stay back as, with a casual swipe of his hand, he tore apart one and then the other of the secure doors leading out of custody. Splinters of glass and wood flew everywhere; Liv shielded herself as she followed.

Officers responding to the urgent assistance call screamed and ducked as debris flew in the air. They ran for cover as the beast ran through the station office and smashed through the screen that covered the front desk.

Liv jumped over what was left of the desk, ducked as Matthew burst through the main entrance of the police station, and threw another dart.

Another scream rang out as she hit him in the back. More shouts and alarms sounded and were drowned out as the creature sprinted out into the night and let out a triumphant howl.

Live stopped and bent over to catch her breath, wincing with the sudden and unexpected effort. She stood up, stared into the night, and looked at the dagger in her hand with the creature's blood on it.

"Bollocks!"

Wednesday morning, 0215 hours

Lauren turned on the blues and twos as she spun the Focus round and headed back to the station.

"This is Foxtrot Oscar one, what's the situation?" Inspector Kent yelled over the radio.

"Matthew Westmore has just escaped from custody. Last seen heading for London Road."

"Silver two, copy," said the TSG Inspector.

"Silver three, got that," echoed the SO19 Inspector.

"This is Silver one. We are nearby on Almond Grove," Inspector Kent said.

"Be advised the suspect is armed and extremely dangerous," Kellie's voice announced. "He turned into something, er, big."

Lauren killed the lights and the sirens and slowed down as they approached the main dual carriageway. The inspector's eyes scanned the houses and the shops, looking for any sign of Matthew. Or something that was a werewolf.

"Well, my dad needs to do a retraction statement," Lauren said as she looked. "That whole werewolves-don't-exist programme seems pretty lame now."

Kent smiled, glad to relieve the tension. Both of them had felt a very real chill when they heard the description of what Matthew had become.

"Murder squad were speaking with Vicky Harper. Maybe we could get her to train him?" Kent said.

Lauren laughed. "So if Amy is bragging about being the blonde suspect and she is the same as Matthew, then that means she really is a bitch!"

They laughed again, and Lauren slowed the car to a crawl and then a stop. Her eyes squinted as they spotted movement down a side alley.

"Foxtrot Oscar from eight-five-five. Movement spotted near Rashid's Fish and Chips."

Kent frowned, unable to see anything. Lauren got out of the car, turning her radio down. Inspector Kent followed her, and they both moved towards Rashid's.

Lauren's heart pounded in her ribcage as she took out her asp but did not extend it. She heard over the radio that TSG and SO19 were on the way to them. Inspector Kent was close behind her as they approached the side alley, and Lauren peered cautiously around the wall.

They were going to wait for the others to arrive before going in. If the chatter coming over the radio was correct, they did not want to be so stupid as to confront him on their own. This was just a recon and follow job.

A few metres away, she saw a figure in the darkness. It turned to look at her, and she caught a flash of blonde fur before the figure ran off up the alley. Lauren ran in, pressing her emergency button.

"Stop, Matthew!" she yelled as he ran away from her.

The two women wanted nothing more than to follow him up the alley, but they had to be cautious. They hesitated and waited. The figure seemed to disappear; however, they could still hear him snuffling down at the end of the alley.

"Matthew!" Inspector Kent snapped.

The figure growled in response.

Lauren let out a frustrated moan and leaned against the wall, gripping it. "What do we do now?" she asked.

The inspector shook her head and got on her radio. "This is Silver one. Suspect has been contained. Repeat, suspect has …"

She trailed off as she looked past Lauren to the road and where their car was parked.

Lauren felt the hairs on the back of her neck prickle. She felt the heat from someone standing right behind her, could feel eyes looking down at her. She flicked open her asp, spun to her left, and whacked him on the side of his body.

He did not flinch. She gazed in horror at the thing before her. He let out a growl of displeasure and swiped his left hand at her.

Lauren turned to run but felt her body slam to the right as he hit her. The force sent her flying into the brick wall, and she fell to the ground, dazed. Her left arm was numb, and she felt a searing pain in her left shoulder and back. Her vision became blurred as she saw the inspector run over to her, talking urgently into her radio.

She watched as the inspector faced the figure, standing up and pulling out her CS spray.

Lauren then realised that the figure in the alley had been a decoy. There were other creatures there, all taller than the first. They surrounded the inspector, who was showing obvious fear and was trying to keep an eye on them all.

Lauren let out an agonised cry as she reached for her radio and felt the blood pour hot down her back.

"Urgent assistance, officer down," she croaked weakly.

The blonde creature lowered his snout until it all but touched the tip of Kent's nose. He breathed in deeply, letting out a soft grumble of pleasure. The inspector raised her face to look him directly in the eyes.

The sound of sirens in the distance became louder as they drew nearer.

The creature seemed to grin as his hand swept up Kent's body, disembowelling her. Lauren felt sick as the creature moved towards her, fangs bared.

Her flesh tingled, and as she blacked out, she heard her own voice, distant and quiet. "Silver one is down …"

CHAPTER THIRTEEN

Wednesday morning, 0310 hours

Ingrid growled angrily as her phone buzzed to life, lights flashing in her darkened bedroom. She rolled over and picked it up from the bedside table and was tempted to hurl it at the wall and smash the damn thing. Automatically she answered it, not checking the caller ID.

The sound of crying met her answer. Ingrid sat up quickly as she heard the inconsolable wailing of the caller, and she spoke softly in reply. She could hear noises in the background – police radios, alarms, and sirens – but the crying overpowered everything. It was terrible, and the sense of grief was overwhelming. She listened to the female voice explain what had happened and then blame herself.

Ingrid got out of bed and paced her room. James was sitting up, alert and full of concern, having woken up at the same time. He could hear what was going on, every word, and his face was awash with sympathy.

"Liv, this is not your fault, love. We're coming to help," she promised.

Reluctantly, Ingrid hung up the phone and ran from her room, not bothering to dress. James would have her clothes out and ready for her when she returned. There were good reasons they were a mated pair.

Ingrid did not bother to knock before swinging open Marcus's bedroom door and marching over to his bed. She did not even have to call out. Marcus sensed her and was awake in a flash; he did not sleep so much as doze. He sat up and looked at her. Ingrid realised she was crying.

"Boss, there's been another one," she started. "The suspect the police arrested broke out of custody an hour ago. He Changed in the cell and broke out." She paused and closed her eyes, gripping her mobile phone so hard that the screen cracked. "He killed a police inspector, Liv's inspector, and mauled another officer."

"Mauled? Bitten?" he asked urgently.

Ingrid shook her head. "Liv says the officer is at the hospital, so she can't verify, but they've just been told about their inspector." She sniffed. "This is terrible. We have to go to them and help them!"

Marcus got out of bed and rested his hands on Ingrid's shoulders. "We will. Go and wake everyone up. I know how close you and Liv are."

Wednesday morning, 0315 hours

The sliding doors of Accident and Emergency opened, letting in a gush of cold air. Jack, wearing jeans and a T-shirt he had thrown on, ran into the reception. He pulled out his warrant card and held it aloft to the receptionist, who was booking someone in. She gave him a look of sympathy and pointed down a corridor.

He trotted along the pale green corridor, the smell of disinfectant barely masking the smell of vomit. He could hear the police radios and made for them. This part of the casualty department was divided into small triage rooms. Outside one of these rooms stood three officers, two he had met at the Beachwood Park murders and one he had seen in the control room.

"DS Ladd," Sergeant Tom Haliday greeted him. He looked pale and drawn as Jack approached and shook his hand.

He could hear screaming from inside the room and looked.

Lauren was on a bed, and nurses were trying to hold her down. She was screaming and looking about wildly, struggling to break free. Blood covered her face, chest, and back, and he could see the claw furrows in her flesh and on her upper arm. Her left shoulder was a mess, and her Met vest was in tatters on the floor, and not due to the medical staff having cut it off.

The casualty doctor looked at him. "Are you family?" she asked urgently.

He stepped into the room. "As close as," he said.

"Good. Is she allergic to anything?"

Jack shook his head. The doctor then barked orders to the others. They managed to pin Lauren down long enough to get a line in and then a sedative. Lauren squirmed and then looked at Jack.

"Silver is down! Silver is down!" she gasped.

He looked at the damage done to her body. As the sedative kicked in, she began to drift off. The doctor shook her head.

"That dose should have killed her," she said, checking her vitals.

Jack looked at Brett and Pete, both of whom had been crying. "What happened?" he asked.

Pete sank down onto a chair. "Matthew escaped, killed the guvnor, and nearly took out Lauren," he said, his voice distant.

Jack rubbed his unshaven chin. "Fuck me, how did he escape?"

Pete looked up at him. "He changed into a fucking werewolf, Sergeant. I saw it with my own eyes, and I don't believe it."

One hour later

Jack finished the call to Lauren's parents and then made his way back into hospital. He stopped at the vending machine in the main waiting area and bought a coffee and then walked towards the room where they had put Lauren. He did not remember the corridor being so long.

Lauren was still asleep and had been pumped full of painkillers. Jack had left a message with her dad's personal assistant and had sat by her side, waiting for him to call back. He watched over her, looked at her injuries, and again got confirmation in his mind that Matthew was the killer. The wounds were the same. What was more, they appeared to be healing. Dressings aside, Jack could see the exposed and ripped skin meld itself back to normal before his eyes. He rubbed his eyes madly, thinking he was seeing things, and then Lauren's Dad called back and Jack took the call, leaving Pete and Brett with her.

Halfway along the corridor, something caught Jack's eye, and he stopped. He looked in another of the rooms and saw a man on the bed, shirtless. He was a middle-aged man, maybe late fifties, and looked careworn under his mop of greying hair. All over his chest and back were cuts very similar to Lauren's injuries.

Jack knocked politely on the door and showed his badge to the man. "Sir, are you OK?" he asked.

Robin looked up at the sound of Jack's voice. He looked at the badge and shook his head. "I'll be fine, officer," he said.

"Forgive me, but you look far from fine. You look as though you've been attacked."

"Well, I haven't."

"I can get an officer to take a report from you. We've got other victims; one of them is a friend of mine. She was attacked by something," Jack prompted. "You can tell me, no matter how strange."

Robin looked at him again. "Nothing happened, officer. I'll be fine," he repeated.

Jack stood there for a few moments, looking at the man and his injuries. The man turned his head away, pointedly ignoring him. Jack sighed, shook his head, and made his way back to Lauren's room.

Marcus let out a colourful tirade of swear words after he hung up the phone. He loathed call centres at the best of times, but this was ridiculous. He had called the main switchboard number for his local police, had been put through to a call centre goodness knew where in London, and had been cut off because the operator thought he was joking when he asked to speak with Detective Sergeant Jack Ladd. He had called back twice more only to be threatened with arrest if he persisted.

Ingrid had left with James and was on the way to get Liv and Sam, who had been sent home along with the rest of their team. There would be no way that either of them would be able to drive.

Marcus in the meantime was trying to get hold of DS Ladd or anyone in CID to arrange a meeting with them. It had proven hopeless.

The sound of a van door sliding shut came to him, and he recognised it as Victoria's. He walked from the living room to the main entrance hallway and out to the front.

Her dark blue van with the picture of her and the sanctuary dogs on the side was parked outside the front door. Stefan placed some static poles and leads in the back and slammed the doors shut. He wore dark blue overalls, and Victoria emerged from the driver's side door wearing the same.

She stopped as she saw Marcus standing there. "Hi, son. What are you doing up?" she asked.

He looked at her incredulously but then remembered that she could sleep through an earthquake. The only thing able to wake her was a call concerning her dogs.

"There has been another incident," he said and then explained what had happened.

Victoria sat on the steps leading up to the front door. "Dear God!" she gasped. "We need to kill them all, Marcus, today!"

Marcus waved his phone. "I've been trying to get in touch with DS Ladd, mother. I'm going to tell him about us and offer our help. It's the right thing to do."

She nodded. "I agree," she said and then sighed. "Grab a set of overalls then."

He frowned. "Why?"

"I got a call from the local council. The police need an animal warden at the station for a briefing this morning at eight. Apparently, they need someone who has experience in dealing with wild dogs," she said.

Marcus breathed a sigh of relief. He leaned over and kissed her cheek. "Bless you and those crazy dogs."

Wednesday morning, 0730 hours

The front of the police station resembled a bomb site. Cordons had been set up around the damaged building itself, and in the street were parked several police carriers with riot shields. Firearms officers stood guard on the front forecourt along with a couple of dog units. There was an atmosphere hanging thickly in the air like a fog, a tension and a sorrow.

Journalists and television cameras recorded everything from the outer cordon as they waited to be escorted into the community centre opposite the station. A press conference was due to be held at nine that morning, and they had already seen the assistant commissioner arrive at the police station.

Uniformed officers and PCSOs patrolled the outer cordon, and every so often a member of the public arrived with a bunch of flowers to be placed in memory of the fallen inspector.

The street where the latest murder had happened was closed off completely, and no access had been allowed. Those who wished to pay their respects made their way to the main police station to deliver cards, stuffed toys, and flowers, which were placed reverently on the front forecourt.

Jack stepped into the cordoned off area which until a few hours ago had been the front office. He had gone home to shower, shave, and put a suit on, as he would be present at the press conference. He had wanted to turn up in a state, to tell the press that he and his colleagues were not fine and everything would not be OK.

It looked like a building site; debris and chunks of wall lay strewn on the floor. Shards of glass were being swept up by men and women working for building services. Crime scene tape hung everywhere, and a small paper sign taped to the front door informed the public that the front office was closed.

A PCSO stood in the mess, checking the warrant cards of all that passed, and mood of the PC and the civilian station reception officer was sombre as the death of one officer and serious injury of another they knew personally sunk in.

The male station officer nodded a greeting to Jack as the DS picked his way through the debris.

"I thought it was bomb-proof glass," he said incredulously.

"It was," replied the station officer. "Well, at least we'll get our front office refurb now."

Jack grinned.

"You ain't seen the CCTV yet," Ted teased as he came through the hole in the wall that had been the secure entry door.

Jack fixed him with his grey eyes. "It can't be any worse than the crime scenes, surely?"

"No, but you won't believe it."

Jack frowned. "This is all we need." He sighed. He moved past the workmen and the PCSO and headed for the CID office. "It's a bloody good job there are plenty of people to stand on these crime scenes," Jack said.

Ted shrugged. "Well, now the commissioner and the assistant commissioner are involved, the box of PCs won't be allowed to run out. Especially after last night."

Jack walked into the CID office and approached the small crowd which had gathered around the large television screen used for displaying CCTV footage. The screen was split into four, and the footage from custody had already been downloaded onto a DVD.

DI Sprite was shaking his head in disbelief. Some of the officers gasped in shock.

"Jesus! Play that again!" he barked to the DC with the remote control.

Jack pushed his way through the officers to stand next to the DI. The DI looked at him and rested a hand on his shoulder.

"How's your mate, Jack?" he asked.

Jack shrugged. "It looked really bad, boss, but when they cleaned her up she just needed some stitches. It was shock mainly, and the injuries will scar, but an early turn unit will be taking her home soon."

"That's good. Who will be with her?"

"I've ordered the early turn unit to stay with her. Their inspector has authorised that until her parents arrive tonight." Jack looked at the television screen. "So, what have we got?"

"I've watched this three times now, and I still can't bloody believe it," DI Sprite told him.

Jack scowled.

The tape was played again and showed a split-screen view of the cell, the corridor outside the cell, the main area of custody, and the main front desk. The scene played out: Matthew stood up, yelled for help, and pounded on the door. Then he ripped off his clothes as though he were on fire, his body dripping with sweat. The chilling screams could be heard once more along with the alarms. Then Matthew changed. His flesh rippled; the vertebrae of his back cracked and stretched. He fell to the concrete floor and writhed in agony as his limbs stretched and swelled. Hair sprouted all over his exposed skin, and his jaw cracked and grew outward, meeting his elongating nose. The voice became a low growl as the rest of his body pulsed and throbbed as he changed.

The creature stood up, taller than before, looked at the door, and charged for it. The door buckled in two hits, and then there was the carnage. Jack watched open mouthed as the officers ducked out of the way and the very small station officer took on the creature and chased him out of the station.

"Shit! Did I just see that?"

DI Sprite glanced at him. "I keep asking myself the same question," he said. "Copies have been made and sent to DPS. I would have loved an independent witness to this though."

"Yeah, where are the custody visitors when you need them?" Jack said. "And who is that station officer?"

DI Sprite grinned. "I know, she's the only one not peeing her pants."

"So Matthew Westmore is our killer," Ted said.

The DI looked at him, and then a look of realisation flashed across his face. "The screwed up DNA! Where's SOCO?"

Victoria showed the armed police officer her council ID. He took it from her, checked it carefully, and then handed it back and waved her through. She thanked him and drove the van to a parking space in front of the station and switched off the engine.

She got out, followed by Marcus, Stefan, and Ingrid, and looked up at the building in front of her with the blue lamp out front. She shuddered slightly and felt apprehensive about being there. It had been years since she had been near a police station, and that last experience had not been good. She was facing her greatest fear, and it was overwhelming.

She then felt an energy reaching out to her, curious and open in the way only a dog could be. Victoria looked to her right and saw the two dog handlers with their German Shepherds. The dogs pointed their snouts at her and sniffed; they then sat back, wagged their tails, and yipped. They were welcoming her to their territory, and it calmed her instantly. If these dogs were happy and relaxed, then there was nothing for her to worry about. The handlers scratched and played with them, giving them fuss, and it reassured her even more.

Victoria took a deep breath and headed for the officer standing outside the station. "Hello, officer, could you please tell your CID that the specialised animal wardens are here for the briefing at eight?"

Jack knocked on the SOCO officer's door. "Boss, the animal wardens are here. An officer is bringing them up."

The DI nodded. He was looking at a sheet of paper in his hand. "Good. Show them the CCTV. I want them to know what we are dealing with, so if they want to back out, they can."

Jack nodded and went over the door to CID and waited for the officer to bring the wardens up. When the council had been called, they had been advised that they needed animal wardens who were able to deal with extremely aggressive animals. They had not been told that the animal was a creature that was not supposed to exist, because for the moment, the police had no idea how to announce that to the world.

Jack could not hide his surprise as he saw the officer approach down the long corridor and saw a familiar black face towering above him. He smiled politely as Victoria, Marcus, Stefan, and Ingrid walked in, all wearing dark blue overalls and carrying a duffle bag each.

Victoria placed her bag on the floor and shook hands with Jack. "Sergeant, nice to meet you again," she said.

She hefted the bag back on her shoulder as Jack escorted them farther into the office and towards the television.

"I wanted to thank you again for giving us access to your CCTV. It was a great help," he said.

"We heard about what happened to your colleagues, Sergeant," Marcus said. "Any help we can give is yours. How is the one who survived?"

Jack looked at him. "She's a very good friend of mine and luckily will only have scars to show for it."

Jack was aware that the CID officers were watching Victoria with a sense of awe. She seemed to ignore the attention, but then she was probably used to it.

"We've got a press conference across the road at nine, but I wanted to show you the CCTV from the police station that was taken at the time of the incident." He looked at each of them carefully. "It is disturbing footage, I'm afraid, and if after seeing it you feel you cannot help us, we will understand."

Victoria's opinion of this flat-foot copper was already good, but it went up a notch at the care in his voice. He genuinely was concerned for them. She could smell that he had been awake all night and could also tell he had been around a lot of blood recently.

She was about to respond when a large man with greying blonde hair marched into the office holding a piece of paper. He stopped when he saw her and blushed.

"Vicky Harper!" he exclaimed. "You're the animal warden?"

She smiled at him and then looked back to Jack.

"Ms Harper, may I introduce my boss, Detective Inspector Richard Sprite," Jack said.

DI Sprite shook hands with her. "It is an absolute pleasure, Ms Harper. You have no idea what a big fan of your show I am," he gushed. "We wanted to get a dog and watched your show and then got a rescue Rottweiler, who is a pussy cat because of your method."

Jack stared wide-eyed at his boss. The DI would pay for this later, he thought with an evil grin.

Victoria pulled out a card from one of her pockets. "Well, bring the dog along on one of our group walks, Inspector. You would be more than welcome."

He took the card gently, as though it were a delicate, precious jewel, and placed it in his pocket. "I will. Thank you. We called the dog Annie; she's wonderful."

"I'm glad. Dogs are wonderful creatures and excellent mirrors for their owners' emotional state."

"Mother," Marcus said very softly.

"Sorry, once the topic moves to dogs, I become distracted. We are here to work and, I believe, to watch some shocking CCTV."

Jack smiled and then moved aside for them to look at the television. The group put their bags down and stood around the screen. Ted set up the footage again and started to play it as Jack walked over to the DI.

"Here, Jack, look at this cocked up DNA," he said, running his finger along the graph. "It isn't cocked up at all. It's a fucking mutation, a chimera of two species that have melded together and become something more."

Jack looked at him blankly. "Chimera? Boss, what are you on about?"

"Come on, Jack. We've both got kids; surely you know about altered DNA and mutant superheroes?"

Marcus watched the CCTV footage with the others, his eyes and ears able to pick up nuances that no ordinary human could. They observed the Change, the breakout, and the escape.

Ingrid leaned forward as Matthew ran from custody. She looked at Ted. "Sorry, mate, can I borrow your control?" she asked.

Ted handed it over without a word. Ingrid paused the footage, rewound it, and then watched it again in slow motion.

"Boss, look at this," she said, leaning close to the screen and pointing.

Marcus followed her finger and saw it step by step – the darts hitting, Liv attacking with the silver blade. Again Ingrid paused it and reran it.

"Look, her slide isn't perfect, but bloody good for a human. You can see she does hamstring him – she didn't miss at all."

Victoria scrutinised it too. "Yes, she did get him." She glanced at Ingrid. "She's very good."

Marcus sighed. "He's an alpha. Robin was right. That's why the silver didn't harm him."

"Holy shit, boss. Liv has been blaming herself for not stopping him." She waved a hand at the screen. "He's a fucking alpha …"

"And only another alpha can kill him," Marcus finished.

They stopped as they realised the entire CID office had fallen silent and everyone was staring at them in astonishment. Jack and the DI watched them warily, both of them wondering what was going on.

Marcus cleared his throat. "Is there an office we can go to? We need to talk."

Jack fell into rather than sat on the chair in the borough DI's office. His skin crawled with pins and needles, and the world around him flashed with colours that did not seem real. His breath rasped in his throat, and he knew he was hyperventilating.

A soft, warm hand enclosed his wrist, and a flask was pressed into his hand. "Son? Are you OK?" a deep, rich voice asked.

Jack took the flask and downed the contents. Brandy, a very expensive one at that. He closed his eyes, and his body shook uncontrollably.

"Son?"

Jack opened his eyes and saw a pair of violet ones looking at him with deep concern. They had thankfully stopped glowing and appeared normal now. He still saw the shine, the glow of the predator in them. Jack nodded and rubbed his face with his hands.

"Give me one good reason why I shouldn't have you all nicked for murder," DI Sprite said.

Marcus stood up and faced the large man. "You said it yourself, Inspector – DNA," he replied.

The DI sat on the desk and looked at the four people in front of him. "What do you mean?"

"The mutated DNA you discovered and originally thought to be contaminated. That sample will not be a match to me or mine," Marcus said.

Jack looked up at him. The body language was completely different from that of the pleasant young man he had met at the mansion; Marcus took charge, and he was very used to doing so. Authority radiated from him, oozed from every pore.

DI Sprite sighed and rubbed his face. "How many werewolves are there?"

"My werewolves did not commit these murders, Inspector. These rogues are not part of my pack, and of them, there are six."

"Matthew and his chums," Jack said quietly.

Marcus glanced at him. "Quite."

"How can I be sure we're safe with your lot? We've already got one bunch picking off the locals. What's to stop you?"

Victoria cleared her throat. "Inspector, these rogues are feral, untrained, and are not anything like pack wolves. We find the very idea of eating humans repellent. Frankly, you all smell really badly."

The DI instinctively sniffed an arm pit and then shrugged. Nothing wrong there.

"Boss, these aren't the killers," Jack said, getting his shaky feet under him. "Matthew and his gang are. You know this."

The DI nodded. "I want samples, and I want them sent to the lab now. Get a car to do it. I don't want anything fancy, just elimination. Agree?"

The four wolves nodded.

"Of course, Inspector. Now will you please let us help you?" Marcus said.

The DI groaned. "We don't have much of a choice, do we?" He moved towards the office door and opened it and then looked back at Marcus. "Come on then. If you're their boss, we need to go upstairs now and tell my boss everything. I'm going to need a fucking drink after this, and I hate the smell of booze!"

Jack watched as the DI escorted Marcus out of the office, muttering and cursing as he went. He then looked at the three who remained.

Victoria gave a smile of sympathy. "Imagine being a very innocent and naive middle-class girl and being told this," she said and then nodded to Stefan and Ingrid. "These two are born wolves. I was Bitten. It helps to breathe, Sergeant."

CHAPTER FOURTEEN

Wednesday morning, 0850 hours

Lauren sat in the back of the response car that had been assigned to drive her home and stay with her. Her back, her left arm, and her left shoulder throbbed with pain, and every time she moved, the stitches pulled. She felt like crap, and the pain killers the hospital had given her had not started to work yet.

All she wanted to do was sleep, and she dozed for seconds at a time, jerking awake every time the car stopped and started again in the heavy traffic.

Kenny was driving the car, and he was flirting with the young girl who was his operator. Lauren could not remember her name; she did not really care.

Kenny stopped the car in the street outside her house. He got out of the car and opened the back door for her and tried to help her out. Despite the pain she felt, she refused his offered hand and managed to climb out of the backseat herself and walk on her own.

Kenny walked beside her as she made her way slowly up the steps that led to her front door. "I'll come over and see you tonight if you like," he offered.

"Go away," she mumbled.

"Lauren, I still love you."

Lauren stopped at her front door and looked up at him. In that moment, he seemed so weak and pathetic to her. It was a very strange sensation, and she wondered if it was the drugs making her high. Kenny towered head and shoulders above her, but he appeared the smaller. Her eyes ran over his exposed throat, and she wanted nothing more than to rip it out. The feeling was so overwhelming that she had to look away.

"Fuck you, Kenny," she said quietly. "You never loved me. You lied to me, and you just wanted to use me."

Lauren opened her front door, stepped into the sanctuary of her home, and closed it on his stunned, idiotic expression. She shuffled into the living room and looked out the front window as Kenny ran back down the steps and got back into the car.

The land line phone began to ring, and she moved awkwardly over to the side table by the sofa where it sat and answered it.

"Hello," she answered in a weak voice.

"We're just waiting for our flight to be called, baby," a deep, familiar voice said. "Are you going to tell me what's going on?"

"Oh, Dad!" she cried. "I don't know where to begin."

Wednesday morning, 0900 hours

The community centre opposite the police station was a reasonable size, with one massive central hall. It was used extensively by help groups and religious groups alike and had been chosen as the best place to host the press conference.

Large display flats had been set up on the raised stage at the end of the hall. They were dark blue in colour with the Metropolitan Police Service crest fixed on them. In front of the flats were tables all in a row covered in dark blue cloth with seating for four people. A glass of water, a microphone, and a name tag had been placed in front of each seat.

Journalists were shown into the main hall by the press officer and escorted to the seats. Camera crews were shown to relative positions around the edge of the hall and allowed to set up.

Assistant Commissioner Christina Taylor stood behind the flats, listening to the press being brought in. Usually she was fine during press conferences and had done a few in her time as second to the police commissioner, but this was different. She had had to rewrite part of her prepared speech after watching the custody CCTV footage and had no idea what the reception would be. She had asked the video unit to prepare some stills and a short section of film to prove her point, which went against procedure somewhat, because internal investigations had not looked at it properly yet. This was something that could not be hidden while they waited for someone in an office to approve dissemination. This was a new and unusual set of circumstances.

She ran her fingers through her short red hair with dyed purple tips and took a deep breath. Christina was wearing her number-one uniform, and it looked immaculate, professional, and together, but she felt anything but. She was a member of the Metropolitan Police Service Women's Society, had pushed at a very young service age to gain promotion quickly, and knew how to play the politics game so well that she could deal with any situation thrown at her. This situation scared the hell out of her.

She looked at the others, the DS and the DI dealing with the murder and the borough commander, who would be up on stage with her, and she was relieved to see they all looked as nervous as she. Then Christina looked at the other person who would remain backstage but ready to come out and assist if necessary.

Christina had grown up reading and researching Victoria Harper and admired her greatly. Victoria Harper was a pioneer for women's rights and equality around the world. As a young, career-minded, gay female in a middle-class family, Christina had found an avenue other than the marriage and family her mother had wanted for her and a woman who understood. She pushed herself forward in university, joined the police, and was on their accelerated promotion scheme, and every year, Christina went to the week-long seminars Victoria held at the Moonscape mansion. She had met her wife there, and they were discussing having children, so in the end, she had managed to have both career and family. One of Victoria's messages was simple: "We are women, we can have it all, and we can take it all."

Victoria smiled at her, giving her encouragement, and Christina returned the gesture. There had been a short briefing before they made their way across the road from the police station, and it had revealed that her idol, Victoria Harper, was actually a werewolf and mother to the current alpha male in the World Wolf Pack. Christina was not surprised once she got over the initial shock. It explained a lot about how strong willed the woman was and why she was so good at dog psychology. It did not change Victoria as a person in Christina's eyes – she had been bitten, not born into it, and apparently had been a protesting feminist before becoming a wolf.

The press officer poked his head around the flat. "Everyone is here, ma'am," he said to her.

She nodded and looked at the others. "Ready?" she asked.

Christina pulled herself taller, tugged at her uniform jacket, and then made her way to the stage and took her seat, followed by Chief Superintendent May, DI Sprite, and DS Ladd. Once they were all seated, Christina glanced at her prepared speech, checked her microphone, and then made the introductions for the others present, explaining their roles in this major incident.

"Before we begin," she said, her voice smooth and clear, "I will read out a prepared statement. Please refrain from questions until after."

She looked at the remote control for the television by her statement and picked both up. Her heart was beating rapidly, and she had never been so nervous in all her life. She paused, took a deep breath, and then began.

"I want to begin by paying tribute to response team Inspector Katherine Kent. Her team and her colleagues feel her loss deeply. She was a hard-working officer, always going above and beyond the call of her duty." She clicked the remote, and the custody photo of Matthew came up on the screen. "You will all be given press packs in a moment; we have withheld them for a reason. This is Matthew Westmore. He was a named suspect in relation to a spate of serious assaults Monday night at Cannon's Bar on the High Street. He was subsequently arrested for these offences and was linked to the victims of the murders which occurred a few days earlier. Matthew Westmore escaped from police custody in the early hours of this morning, and during the manhunt for him, he attacked and killed Inspector Katherine Kent and seriously injured PC Lauren Wylie." She paused, took a sip of her water, and tried to stop the trembling. She glanced to her side and saw Victoria standing in the shadows, a proud smile on her face. Christina cleared her throat. "Matthew Westmore is a very strong suspect for the murders. He is not to be approached and is extremely dangerous." This was it; she could feel the trepidation of the three men sitting up there with her. "Matthew Westmore suffers from a rare and unusual condition which transforms him and gives him an abnormal level of strength." She clicked the button on the remote, and a small portion of the CCTV played out, showing Matthew Changing. "Matthew Westmore is a werewolf."

The members of the press watched the footage in horror. There was a moment of shocked silence and then an insane cacophony of screams, shouts, and questions.

Wednesday afternoon, 1230 hours

The mood was sombre. They had been sent home from night duty, but they could not sleep, and all they seemed capable of doing was cry. The floods of tears came and then drifted away only to come back again minutes or hours later. They could not sleep, so a few of them met up in a pub by the river and sat around a table staring numbly into their respective drinks. When the bout of tears hit, they held onto each other, a support through the latest storm; then they went back to gazing into space, thoughts tumbling through their minds.

Ingrid had asked James to stay with them and look after them, so when they had agreed to meet their teammates at the pub, he had gone along and bought the drinks. He did not know what he was expecting, but he was greeted with quiet chatter and, surprisingly, the odd funny story about life on a response team.

The atmosphere in the pub was strange; the big-screen television, usually broadcasting the latest football, was showing the press conference on a loop via a news channel. The other patrons of the pub seemed to be taking the announcement that werewolves existed surprisingly well: some were afraid; others outed various celebrities as werewolves.

James received a call on his mobile phone and left the table to go outside and take it.

"How are they?" Ingrid asked when he answered.

James sighed. "I wish there was something I could say or do. There is so much pain here," he said. "What's happening there?"

"We're about to start the briefing for the wolf hunt," she said. "I have to say, they took the news about the whole werewolf thing very well for human police. Vicky is in her element. She has just been out in the yard with the dog units, and I've been playing with the TSG. I love some of the toys they get."

"My love, you do not need toys; you have claws," he said and could hear her smile.

"I know. You need to explain something to Liv. Even though her moves need a little work, the rogue escaping from her was not her fault," Ingrid said. "The wolf was an alpha, and she did not miss."

James sighed. "Thanks, honey. That will go some way to making her feel better. I think she will still blame herself though."

He could hear voices in the background. "Listen, I have to go," she said. "Love you."

"Love you too."

He hung up the phone and went back into the pub. He took his seat next to Liv and Sam, and he looked at her.

"That was Ingrid," he explained. "The pack is helping with the search for Matthew. She also wanted me to tell you that he was an alpha."

Liv nodded as she understood. "I knew I didn't miss the fucker," she said.

Pete frowned from his side of the table. "What's an alpha?"

"Basically the leader of the pack; they are the strongest by nature, and they are resistant to silver," he said and then looked pointedly at Liv. "And only another alpha can kill them. It wouldn't have mattered how many times Liv hit him with her weapons; they would not have brought him down."

Liv shrugged. "I am still to blame though," she said.

Sam squeezed her hand. "No, you're not, Liv. You weren't allowed to tell anyone about being a hunter. You would have been sectioned in the mental ward for sure."

Andrew leaned forward. "No one saw this coming, Liv. No one."

"But I knew it was a pack of rogues committing the murders. I should have spoken up!"

Sam put an arm around her and held her close. He looked around the table and then at James. "So what is happening now?"

"We help track the wolves, and either your lot will capture them or we will take them out," he said bluntly.

Brett took a swig of his pint. "I'm for the latter," he said.

There were murmurs of agreement.

Liv stood up. "I'm going there to help," she said. "I want to be part of the hunt."

Pete nodded. "So do I, but they won't let us, Liv. They've got no idea what they're dealing with, and they won't want us bugging them."

"Then I won't go as police staff; I'll go as a hunter. I know what they are dealing with and how to deal with it more than bloody TSG do." She looked around the table. "I'm going to pick up my extensive collection of weapons, and I am going to hunt down that rogue pack and make them pay for what they have done."

Wednesday afternoon, 1330 hours

Victoria felt like someone who had spent her entire life afraid of heights, had then done a bungee jump, and was now an adrenaline addict. She sat in the writing room on the ground floor of the police station and watched it slowly fill with uniformed officers.

Ingrid sat with the TSG officers, looking at their riot gear and discussing its usage in real-life situations. She hefted the enforcer easily and then wielded it with one arm with the circular shield in the other to impressed looks from the massive officers, who needed both arms to swing it. She pointed out that her method of entry to a house was to just boot the door in. The officers of longer service bonded with her immediately; as head of security for the pack she had a lot in common with them, and they picked up on that.

It had been the dog unit for Victoria, that and the assistant commissioner. Victoria had recognised her from the seminars about women in business she gave every year, and while they had waited for everyone to arrive for the main briefing they had stood out in the yard chatting with the dog units and, more importantly for Victoria, the dogs.

Then Marcus, the AC, the DI, and the DS had gone into an office with the inspectors from TSG and SO19 to discuss points of the briefing. Victoria may have been requested as an animal expert, but now that the truth was out, Marcus, as pack leader, would run point for the werewolves.

Victoria returned with Stefan to the writing room and sat with the waiting officers. One of them enquired as to how many dogs had tried to hump her leg and how he could stop them doing that to him when he went to a house. The humour was a balm to them; they were in pain and heartbroken at the loss of one of their own, but she found it incredible how these officers picked themselves up, brushed themselves down, and continued on with their jobs. The joking around was a way to deal with the horrors they witnessed every day.

Her nose went into overdrive at the excitement in the air, and the boisterous behaviour was just another sign of that. A few of the early turn response officers who had what was called level three training, equivalent to the TSG, were also in the room, and Victoria could smell crime scenes on some of them. One, a male officer, had obviously been at the scene where the inspector had been killed, as she could smell blood and one of the rogues.

The door to the writing room opened, and Marcus walked in, followed by the senior officers. They all stood at the front of the room before a massive map of the area pinned to the wall. Marcus looked at the map, took a red pen from the stationary desk, and began to draw borders on it. He then looked at the waiting officers.

Christina stepped forward. "Afternoon, troops. This briefing is going to be started by Marcus Siguardulfsen. He, as you now know, is the alpha male of the pack. He will explain a few things to you and rules of engagement, and then we will discuss RVPs and the best place to start the search."

She looked at Marcus and nodded. Officers then pulled out pocketbooks and prepared to take notes.

"Good afternoon," he began. "My people have conducted a partial investigation of this matter. We take the attack and killing of humans very seriously, and this crime carries the death penalty. My head of security was able to discern that it was six rogues in total. They are not members of my pack and were turned against my knowledge and our laws. We can start the search by tracking the scent of Matthew from custody." He looked carefully over each face in front of him. "No one – I repeat, no one – is to approach Matthew Westmore. He is an alpha, and only I can take him on. My people will distribute silver weapons to you all. Again, these will not work on Matthew but will work on the others."

Marcus stepped back, and the TSG inspector stepped forward. He pointed at the map and the area Marcus had marked in red. "This area here is covered by Lunar Park and surrounding estates. As Marcus here is an alpha, this rogue pack will not go into his territory. His people will start the search, one of them in each carrier." He then handed out some sheets of paper to the officers. "Here is a list of potential rendezvous points in the borough, covering as many places as we can. Each location will change as the tracking continues. The procedure will be to track, to meet up, and to track again. I do not want anyone charging ahead."

DI Sprite then took his turn. "This has been a very tough week for this borough, and I want minimum civvie involvement with this. The press conference is going to have everyone crapping themselves and jumping at nothing. We need to be calm and follow to the letter every order issued by Marcus and his people. You don't follow their orders, you will be sent back to the police station and put on report. When the tracking is done and we locate the rogue pack, Marcus and his people will change and combat the others. The pack wolves will be a lot larger than these rogues, but do not interfere when they fight. If we get in their way, the rogues will kill us without thinking twice about it, so again, follow orders."

He pointed to photographs pinned to the board next to Matthew. "Take a look at these photos. They are not recent; however, they are all friends of Matthew and were in his drug therapy group. The first one, Amy Farringdon, is his girlfriend. Werewolf aside, she is psychotic. She murdered her baby brother at the age of ten, but social services believed her story when she said she hugged him too tight. At the age of eleven, she seriously injured her mother. A year later she was pregnant. She says that the father left, but from the amount of his blood in the room, he has to be dead. We have not found his body. We sent a unit to her mother's house and unfortunately found her body in pieces. Amy killed her about two weeks ago, and no one knew.

"Next we have Inderjit Kaur. From a very nice family and good upbringing, but she got hooked on drugs, and her family disowned her after they found out she was seeing Craig Pratchett, who is the next one on our list.

"That leaves Thomas Cregan and Daniel. Daniel is the one who escaped, so we don't have any information on him, and it seems he was not part of the therapy group. The people in the shopping centre and the High Street stores have been given his photo and told to call us if he is seen anywhere. However, he seems to have vanished."

Jack then looked around the room. "Lauren is my mate," he said. "I know a lot of you work with her or know her or her dad. She was very, very lucky to survive with just a few scars. Lauren is cautious, not given to being stupid and rushing in, and Matthew almost gutted her too. Follow the orders of the pack, and let's get these fuckers for Lauren and Inspector Kent."

There were mumblings of approval in the room.

The briefing broke up, and the officers filtered out of the writing room and made their way to the carriers parked out front. Jack walked with Marcus and the others towards the custody suite and stood by the door.

"Be careful stepping in there; it's still a bit of a wreck," he said and pointed through the two broken doors. "Camera cell one is down the corridor to the right, and it's the first door." He laughed. "Well, it's the broken one."

Marcus grinned and patted Jack on the arm. "Don't worry, we'll figure it out."

Jack watched and waited as the wolves picked their way through the debris and trotted down the corridor. He found it strange that he automatically thought of them as wolves rather than humans, but it was easy. They made no sound at all as they moved, and they glided with a smooth elegance he was envious of.

After a few minutes they came back, and Jack squirmed uncomfortably as he saw their glowing eyes return to normal.

"We have what we need, Sergeant," Marcus said.

They walked out of the custody area and joined the officers waiting outside.

Liv stood on the front forecourt flanked by James, Sam, and the other officers from her team. Her light brown hair was pulled back into a pony tail; her hazel eyes were cold and hard. She wore a grey T-shirt, jeans, and boots with a three-quarter-length brown leather jacket that looked a little too big for her. She carried a large case, and her silver bowie knife was hooked on her belt. She looked every inch the hunter.

The officers stared at Liv and her teammates, and no one seemed to know what to say. Ingrid saw the pain on Liv's face and stepped forward. She reached out to Liv and Sam and hugged them to her. James joined in, and soon silent hugs were exchanged with everyone there.

Liv lifted her case. "I brought Betty with me," she said.

Ingrid looked at Marcus. "I'm having her on my bus," she said.

Jack looked out the side door of the carrier and watched Marcus. Marcus was a few feet ahead of the bus and was crouched on the ground, sniffing the air. He nodded, jumped back in the vehicle, and gave the new directions to an officer holding a tablet. The computers were provided by Moonscape and were ten times faster than the Met issue ones. The officer drew the lines on the map, and Marcus took a look at the results as the other teams updated their results and they popped up on the screen in a different colour.

It was slow going, as the wolves got out and checked the scent every few minutes. Jack observed how the TSG and shield trained officers had adapted to this. They were used to all the waiting around, as a lot of the time that's what happened on a level-three day. It was only when a situation went bad that they were called in; until then it was a waiting game.

Some of the officers played cards, another played a game on his smart phone, and one of the female officers was doing crochet in her full riot gear. It was a very surreal scene, one he was sure was repeated on the other carriers.

Brett watched Liv as she opened the large case she carried and started to put together the black and silver compound bow. She had taken off her jacket, and he could see how muscular her arms were. The police staff uniform was not exactly complimentary to any human body, but it had hidden a lot about Liv's. Once she strung the bow and checked the sights, she counted the arrows and made sure the tips were in good order.

"So the press up competition we had during early turn when you only managed four full ones – were you faking?" he asked her.

She looked at him and grinned. "Yes," she admitted.

"How many can you do?"

She shrugged. "I've never counted. My fitness isn't about vanity or a figure; it's for survival."

He looked at the very large silver knife she had given him. "I'm terrified."

"Good, means you're not arrogant enough to make a mistake and get us killed," she said.

Brett smiled. She seemed to be a completely different person from the one he knew from work. Liv had been giving pointers to the officer about the best places to strike if they got close enough to a werewolf and was recommending they split into small groups of three in order to tackle one of them. She took charge – after all, this was something she was used to and knew a lot more about than they did. Her authority had been confirmed when she introduced them to Betty the Compound Bow.

"I named her after my grandmother; she was one feisty old bat you did not want to get on the wrong side of," she had said to laughter.

Ingrid jumped back on the bus and updated the results. "We need to go to the meet point here," she told the driver, indicating on the map.

She then called the others up on the radio and asked them to join her at the meeting point.

Liv looked at Ingrid as she sat next to her. "They've settled," Liv said.

Ingrid nodded and then looked out the window at the setting sun. "Now we get ready to go and play."

Marcus circled an area on his map and sent it to the various smart phones and computers belonging to those around him. "We've tracked the rogues to this area," he said. "Now, looking at the location on the map, it is safe to assume they are hiding in the park opposite the residential street I have marked. Ingrid and the others are a few streets away in this perimeter." He drew another circle. "We can keep them contained here and will know if they move, which for the last hour they have not."

Jack looked at the marked areas on his smart pad screen. He double-checked it and then felt his blood run cold. "Are you sure these rogues are there?" he asked.

"Certain," Marcus replied. "Why do you ask?"

"Because that's Lauren's street," Liv said.

"She is the officer who was injured, yes?" Marcus asked and received nods from Jack and her teammates.

"Is it possible they have gone back to finish the job?" Jack asked.

Marcus shook his head. "No, otherwise those men Matthew injured at the pub would be dead. There is no reason for the rogues to meet up and wait there." He looked around at the officers as they stood around him, waiting for the next move. He looked at Jack. "Are you sure she was not bitten?"

"I only saw her at the hospital, but as I told you, she was ripped up pretty bad, but I couldn't see any bite marks."

Brett stepped forward. "Me and Pete were first on scene, and I gave her first aid. She was so badly mauled that I couldn't tell."

Marcus looked grim. "If she has been bitten, this changes things. It means they are there to claim her as one of their own."

Jack's face hardened. "Which means what, exactly?" he growled.

"It means she will Change tonight and become a member of their pack."

Jack stepped forward and faced the officers. "Right, I want units on a silent approach at each end of her street. A unit has been assigned to her house, and I want them contacted."

Marcus smelled the air. "Sergeant, there is no police unit in that street," he said.

Jack stopped and looked at him. "What! How do you know?"

"We're half a mile away. Ingrid is closer, and she says the street does not have a police presence. She believes that's why they chose that park to hide in – because they know we are coming."

Jack got on the radio to the control room. "Hi there," he said, his voice tight with anger. "Could you please personal call the officer who was assigned to sit outside PC Wylie's home address, urgently. Activate the radio under authorisation of Operation Clearwater."

They all waited for the control room to get back to them. One of the radios sprang to life in the crowd of waiting officers.

"Six-five-eight, are you receiving on this channel, over!"

Jack glared at the officer; he then contacted the control room again. "Thank you, Foxtrot Oscar, we have the officer here," he said, not taking his eyes from the man in front of him.

He walked over to him. "Well, officer, why are you not outside PC Wylie's house?" he asked.

The scent of anger from Jack was so pungent that Marcus wanted to sneeze. He softly stepped up beside the detective sergeant, whom he had grown rather fond of, ready to intervene quickly if necessary.

Kenny looked at the murder squad officer. "A call for a robbery came out, and we went to deal with that," he explained.

"You were assigned to a call already and not in a position to deal with another one. In fact, you were specifically told not to leave her house. Try another excuse."

"She did not want the unit there, and she told us to go, so the way I saw it, we were better dealing with calls than babysitting someone who did not want us there," Kenny reasoned.

Jack clenched his fists. He glanced at Lauren's teammates and saw the anger on their faces. "It was not up to her, or you. You were given an order!" He was aware his voice was rising with each word.

Kenny pulled himself up. "She told me to fuck off, Sarge. She didn't want me there. I even offered to come and spend the evening with her, but she just swore at me and told me to get lost."

Jack scowled. "Hang on a minute – you're the fucking arsehole who dumped her over the phone the other night," he said.

"What! Impossible," Liv said. "Lauren wouldn't go out with a dick like him!"

Jack nodded. "Lauren told me everything about you when you were together. And it was all lies. You used her. She was attacked by a werewolf, and now, because you left her unprotected, a whole pack of them are outside her house waiting to do God knows what."

"She told me to go!" Kenny yelled.

Jack pulled back his arms to hit the arrogant twat, but Marcus touched his shoulder and stopped him.

The short, stocky blonde chief inspector from TSG marched up to Kenny. "Get back to the fucking station now and contact your federation rep. I am placing you on immediate suspension for disobeying a direct order that has resulted in the life endangerment of another officer. Now fuck off!"

Another officer stepped forward and escorted Kenny away. Jack turned to Marcus.

"Thanks for that, mate," he said. "I do not want to get into trouble for hitting an arsehole like him."

"I realised that, Sergeant," Marcus said. "We need to talk."

Jack and Marcus moved away from the crowd of officers.

"Sergeant, if your friend has been bitten, she will Change any minute now." He sighed. "For those of us born into the pack, the first Change is traumatic, but we are prepared for it all our lives. Those that are Bitten are also prepared; they have to live within the pack for at least five years before the Bite. They see others Change, and they have some idea what to expect, but again, this is traumatic."

"Lauren is a strong person; she will be fine."

Marcus shook his head. "No, she will not. The Change is the most horrific thing a human body can endure, regardless of strength. If she does Change, she will want to die, the pain will be so bad. I can help her deal with this, but if she chooses death, I will let her go."

Jack shook his head. "No, you can't. You must save her."

Marcus could see the tears in his eyes. "It will not be your choice; if I am guiding her and she wants to let go, I cannot hold her back."

A series of haunting howls began to echo in the air. It started with one, and then others joined in to make a beautiful, ethereal song.

Marcus started and sniffed the air.

"Are they yours?" Jack asked.

"No, they are not. We need to go. Now!"

CHAPTER FIFTEEN

Wednesday evening, 1930 hours

Lauren snapped open her eyes and sat up quickly. Dreams, very strange and unusual dreams that she knew were just her mind playing tricks on her. The last one had been about Kenny. He had been in the writing room at work and had been telling everyone how he had made a fool of her. She knew what police officers were like for gossip, and everyone was lapping up his story, and he was laughing about how easy she had been to deceive. She felt such a wave of anger that she marched up to him and hit him. Only it was not her hand; she had claws, and she gutted him.

As she lay back down she thought that her father would have a wealth of theories and explanations about that one.

The high from the pain medication given to her by the hospital provided a thick, foggy shield that she was grateful for. Just out of reach, she could feel the pain in her back and shoulder throbbing faintly. Emotionally, though, she felt wrung out and drained, and a feeling of utter desolation consumed her.

Lauren knew the dream about Kenny was just an expression of her anger at herself for believing his lies. However, it did not matter what her sensible head knew; what he had done still hurt, and in some ways it was worse than the physical pain, because she could not dull it with drugs.

Through the thick drug blanket that covered her senses, a sound came to Lauren, so faint that she was not sure if it was real or part of her delusions. Lying on the sofa in her living room, she strained to hear but found it made her feel dizzy, almost like being drunk.

She heard the sound again – a breath, close to her, from someone in the room with her. Her eyes swivelled in the darkness of the room, and she felt a jolt of excited pain and did not know why.

Matthew Westmore's face appeared in the darkness above her. Lauren opened her mouth to scream, but his left hand closed around her throat, and she stopped as a wave of intense heat flooded through her. She found herself gasping at his touch, having never felt anything like it before in her life.

Matthew's face hovered over hers, handsome and full of life. His blue eyes sparkled with vitality, and Lauren felt drawn to them. Then Matthew kissed her deeply and shocks of electricity jumped through her body, making her tingle to the tips of her toes. The wonderful fog of the pain killers left her abruptly, but so did all the pain from her injuries, gone in an instant, as though it had never been.

Slowly, still kissing her, Matthew pulled her up into a sitting position. Then he pulled away and studied her. Lauren panted for breath but felt energised and wide awake. Everything was crystal clear to her, as though she had just been rebooted and decluttered. She could feel something roll in her, itching to get out. Her skin just felt wrong, and she wanted to rip it all off.

Matthew nodded. "Yes, you are my alpha."

Lauren threw her head back and screamed.

The man opened the front door of his house at the sound of repeated, urgent knocking. On his doorstep stood a uniformed officer in a dark blue jump suit with three silver pips on each shoulder.

"Good evening, sir. I am Chief Inspector Smith with the Tactical Support Group," he said. "We're informing local residents that we have a very dangerous firearms incident about to happen, and we are advising people to move to their back rooms and stay clear of their windows until it is over."

The man looked along the street and saw several officers at other houses all along his road and more police vehicles than he had ever seen in his life.

"Why should I? You can't tell me what to do!" the man protested.

The chief inspector shrugged. "No, but I can make a record of your refusal, and if you and your family are caught in the crossfire, it will be your fault, not ours."

The chief inspector started to march away. The man ran down the steps after him.

"You can't speak to me like that! I pay your wages! Who is your supervisor?" he demanded.

The chief inspector stopped and turned back. "Sir, have you seen the news today? Did you watch the press conference?"

The man nodded.

"Get back in your house. Stay in the back rooms and clear of the windows."

A howl rent the night air from the park across the road. The man paled, ran back into his house, and slammed the door.

Marcus pointed along the street. "We need two lines of officers at each end. We have them contained in the park, but they won't stay there."

He stopped as another howl echoed over the park. The officers were visibly spooked as they hefted their full-length oblong riot shields and asps that had been sprayed with silver and prepared to form their lines.

The sound of screaming came to them, and they all turned towards the park. An Indian woman wearing a track suit covered in blood ran towards them, screeching at the top of her voice. Two TSG officers ran into the middle of the road to meet her, and she collapsed in their arms, tears streaming down her puffy face.

"My dog! My dog!" she wailed.

"What happened, madam?" one of the officers asked.

She gestured and pointed towards the park. "I was walking my Jack Russell in there," she gasped. "Then something took him!"

She started to scream again, and some of the other officers started towards the park. Marcus stepped towards the woman and cursed.

"Officers, get back!" he yelled. "She's one of them!"

The two officers looked at the helpless, traumatised woman on the ground between them and exchanged concerned glances.

Inderjit struck. She grabbed both men by their necks and stood up, bringing them with her. They tried to struggle and strike out at her, but she held firm, claws digging into their flesh slightly. She met Marcus's eyes with a cold hard glare and grinned as she pulled one officer in front of her. Her fangs glistened in the light of the street lamps, and she bit down on the officer's neck. He screamed for a moment as she threw back her head and his blood shot up into the night sky. His colleague struggled in her hold as he saw his friend thrown to the side, but the woman was too strong. Her hand cupped his head, gripped, and pulled. His head popped off wetly, and she threw it at the terrified officers.

Spreading her arms wide, she let out a primal cry to the heavens, and then she turned and bolted back into the park.

The remaining officers gave chase, but Marcus halted them.

"Get back in line! She is luring you out!"

With extreme reluctance, the other members of TSG stopped and bunched together, forming a clumsy line of shields that clacked and trembled together as the terror of those that held them manifested.

Then came the sound of claws scratching along metal, and they winced. The sound squealed in the air and sent shivers up spines. It seemed to come from all around them and not from the park at all.

Marcus stood behind the police line on his end of the street, knowing that Ingrid would be doing likewise at the other end. The screeching stopped, and the growling started. Officers screamed and ducked as a police car sailed over their heads and landed in the middle of the road, bounced, and rolled to a stop mere feet from them. A massive white wolf landed on the upturned vehicle. Police lights shattered as the roof of the car was crushed.

The wolf crouched, whipped his head around, and snarled at the officers, saliva dripping from his huge sharp teeth. Then he launched himself into the air and hit the shield line. The line broke, and officers fell to the ground, weapons and equipment scattering, and the wolf ran off back into the park and howled again, taunting.

The line recovered and the officers surged forward. Marcus shouted at them.

"No! You must stay where you are!"

He could see how hard it was to obey, but they gathered together again.

A flash shot from the park and struck the end of the line. Screams rent the air as body parts flew and shields shattered.

"Circle!" Marcus yelled.

They pulled into formation, facing out through their shields. Marcus pounced in front of them as a white van flew straight towards the officers. He ran to meet it and braced as the weight hit him. Marcus hefted the van easily in his powerful arms and tossed it to the side out of the way. He glared into the darkened park and snarled low, making sure they could hear his challenge.

Lauren kicked Matthew in the stomach and threw him off her. He crashed into the bookcase against the wall, and it shattered, ornaments and books flying apart. She leapt off the sofa and ran for the door, but Matthew recovered and launched himself at her, tackling her, and they both landed on the television unit, which exploded in a cloud of splinters and glass.

He grabbed her by the wrists, and she felt a wave of heat wash over her. She pulled away from him, but the heat did not leave her. It intensified, and she screamed in agony as her body began to burn. Sweat poured over her, and the searing pain got worse and worse. The touch of cloth on her body was like a thousand daggers piercing her skin, flaying the flesh from her bones. She ripped at her clothing, gasping in agony and terror. As the air hit her naked body, she sobbed. She wanted to die so the pain would end.

Another scream sounded, but it did not come from Lauren. Matthew turned quickly to the door as Amy ran into the room. Her face was twisted with fury, and she flew at Lauren. Both of them sailed over the sofa.

Jack clambered up the side of the carrier and reached his hand down for Liv. She passed up her bow and then her arrows and grasped his hand so he could pull her up. They stood on the roof of the riot vehicle and looked at the scene before them.

The TSG had formed a line and were holding firm, and at the other end of the street, the officers there had done the same thing. They wielded their silver asps, ready for any rogue that came near them.

The rogues seemed content with goading them, trying to get them into the park. Their inspectors took over from the pack wolves and shouted instructions, and the officers slipped easily into the familiar discipline. The carrier drivers had repositioned their vehicles and lit their lamps, casting eerie silhouettes over the park.

The rouges had ripped out the wrought-iron fencing from the park and now launched pieces of it at the officers, trying to spear them. A tree had been uprooted and tossed into the waiting lines only to be caught by Ingrid and James. Ingrid partially transformed in front of them, roaring for them to come and face her, colouring the air with her profane curses.

As debris, bins, and cleaved branches bounced off the shields, the officers could fool themselves into believing they were in a normal riot situation, where kettling was the key – contain and control.

Liv held her bow and scanned the shadowed park, an arrow nocked and ready for a target to shoot. Jack stood by her side, her bag of arrows slung over his shoulder and two in his hands, ready to pass them to her. He trembled with fear as he saw the bombardment below him and then jumped as the white wolf jumped into the fray again.

Matthew jumped over the sofa and pulled the woman from the red wolf. He grabbed Amy by her long blonde hair and struck her hard. Blood erupted from the gashes he made as his claws tore her face. He dragged her across the floor away from Lauren. She screamed again and grabbed for his hands. He lifted her into the air, her feet dancing, and he threw her against the wall, buckling the brickwork.

Amy cried out in anger, and her green eyes glowed as she started to Change. The red wolf stood and looked around the room and then yelped as the blonde wolf leapt again and landed on top of her. Yips and growls sounded as they started to fight. The blonde wolf chased and bit into the flank of the large red wolf.

Lauren cried out in pain as she felt the fangs sink deep and fell to the floor. Amy let her go and moved to stand over her. There was a sardonic joy to the green wolf's eyes as her teeth hovered above Lauren. Lauren was terrified. Time seemed to stretch as Amy latched onto her throat and pinned her down.

Lauren felt an incredible power surge through her. She was suddenly aware that she felt very calm and acutely aware of everything around her. She could hear the sound of fighting outside, and something told her she had to get out there. The teeth started to bite down, and Lauren struck. This was her house, her territory, and no psychotic junkie girl was going to take it from her.

She got her feet under Amy's stomach and shoved as hard as she could. The blonde wolf flew into the air and hit the wall. She recovered quickly, landing on all four paws, and snarled viciously at Lauren. Lauren sprang to her paws and stood, hackles raised, growling back, the low reverberation rumbling in her throat. She pounced, landing on the blonde's back and nipping. Quickly, she realised she was stronger than Amy. Her teeth closed in around the soft flesh of the pointed ear and she tore it off. She heard a yelp and felt the energy drain from her attacker as her larger, more dominant jaw gripped the other by the neck and held on, ignoring the pathetic struggles of the blonde wolf.

Amy whined and fell to the floor. Lauren did not let go. Then the red wolf pulled back as the other rolled onto her back and bared her neck, tail twitching between her legs.

Marcus ran back to the carrier, took his clothes off, and threw them into the bus. He flexed, took a deep breath, and went to all fours. He cried out as his muscles and bones ripped and cracked and then knitted together again. He felt his senses become sharper, the smells stronger, and the sheer strength increase in his entire body. Twisting his neck and limbs, he warmed up and then ran for the shield wall.

Smoothly, he soared over it and landed in front of the white wolf. He bared his teeth and threw his head back and howled.

On the bus, Jack covered his ears with the pain of the sheer volume and glanced at Liv.

"Now that is a pack howl," she said.

Jack looked back. Marcus in wolf form was massive, much larger than the white rogue wolf, and the assertive energy rolling from him felt like a solid wall.

Again Marcus howled, longer this time, and the pitch changed into a beautiful song. Claws clacking on the tarmac road could be heard, and three more wolves turned up: Ingrid, a golden brown; Stefan, his ebony coat glossy in the moonlight; and James, a dark grey. Jack saw Victoria behind the other shield wall, still in human form.

The three pack wolves stood behind Marcus, glaring at the white rogue, ready to attack. Marcus paced and growled low, challenging the rogues.

James was struck from the side and slammed into the shield wall. Officers braced but were knocked back, and some fell to the ground. James sprang back up and flew at the grey rogue who had hit him. They rolled around the street, snarling and biting at each other. Ingrid joined in, snapping at the legs of the grey. James latched onto the hindquarters, Ingrid the neck, and they both pulled and worried. A sickening popping sound could be heard as they grey was pulled apart. Ingrid shook her head, ensuring the thing was dead, and then began to circle the white wolf, blood dripping from her snout.

Marcus stood staring down the white as Ingrid circled. Stefan chased a dark brown wolf towards the park, cut her off, and chased her back to the street. James and Stefan wore the female down, nipping and running, nipping and running. The dark brown female panted and collapsed by the entrance to the park and looked up at Stefan and James. The pack wolves went to trot away but stopped as they heard a yelp behind them.

Liv lowered her bow and nocked another arrow. The dark brown female had been shot through the heart and killed mid pounce. Both males yipped at her and ran back towards the pack.

The white wolf stamped his paws and barked at Marcus, lips curling, teeth bared. Ingrid stopped circling and sat down, looking at him. James and Stefan moved in and waited. Marcus moved forward and sniffed the white wolf. Then, in one quick movement, Marcus pinned the white wolf and ripped his stomach open. Blood and guts flew in the frosty air.

The pack wolves then threw back their heads, and the wolf song of triumph began. It was ululating, haunting, and exquisite. The night rang with it, and it floated on the air for miles around.

The red wolf looked down at the subordinate on the floor beneath her. This creature had had the audacity to come into her home and try to kill her. The red wolf sniffed the air as a series of howls echoed outside, and she felt peace wash over her. Those howls belonged to something wholesome and wonderful. She moved her snout over the blonde, and her lip curled in distaste. Then she struck and ripped the throat out.

The red wolf turned slowly to the other repellent creature who had invaded her space. The howls outside called to her, and she wanted to go with them but felt herself tethered to this one. She had to break his hold on her. She snarled as he began to Change, and she ran at him. He grabbed her, and they flew through the air and crashed through the living-room window.

The pack wolves spun at the sound of breaking glass and dodged out of the way as two more wolves landed on the street. One was a pale blonde; the other was far larger and a beautiful coppery red colour. They landed heavily on the ground, the pale blonde one on top. He got off the red wolf as she bit his stomach, and they circled each other, each attempting to stare the other down. The red wolf pounced forward and barked, hackles raised.

Matthew jumped at her, and Lauren dodged to the side, making him slam into the pavement again, and he yelped. He went to get back up, but she body-slammed him, rolled with him, and then gripped the back of his neck with her powerful jaws and shook her head. There was a stomach-churning crack, and Matthew went limp. She dragged him with her teeth, lifted him, and smashed his body on the concrete again, feeling more bones break.

She stepped back and felt the energy of the others there. Her ears pressed back onto her head, and she ran back into the sanctuary of her house.

Marcus flung his jeans back on as Jack and Liv climbed back down from the top of the carrier. "I'm going in there," he said. "You can follow if you wish, but keep your distance."

His bare feet slapped nimbly on the road as he ran over to Lauren's house and took the steps leading up to her door three at a time. He ran along the hall and halted as he reached the wreck that was her living room.

She sat in the corner behind the sofa and stared anxiously around her. Her eyes rolled, her fur stood on end, and she panted. Marcus stepped forward softly but not cautiously. She licked her lips and stamped her front paws, snarling to warn him off.

Marcus smoothly sat by her side, not facing her, and radiated calmness. Lauren stopped snarling, and he could hear her licking her lips again. Then she began to whine, and he felt her cold nose touch his naked shoulder. He moved closer to her. The whining became worse, and she collapsed to the floor and went into convulsions.

Marcus lay next to her as her body bucked and jerked, claws scratching at him. He held on as her body broke itself again and the whine turned to something somewhere between a growl and a scream. Then he began to whisper softly in her pink human ear.

Lauren was dying. She knew this because everything was quiet and still.

She floated in darkness, and there was no pain, no fear, no doubt. There was only peace as she hovered in the abyss. She felt nothing but the moment, the clarity, the purity.

Then she heard the screaming and winced. Whoever it was had to be in agony. It pulled at her, and on one level she knew she was the one who was screaming and on another she did not care anymore.

Lauren sighed as she heard the most beautiful voice whisper in her ear.

"Lauren," he said softly, and the voice made her quiver. It was smooth and deep, suited for reciting poetry or Shakespeare. "You can let go if you wish," he whispered. "Let the pain leave you. Or you can stay."

Lauren frowned. There was a choice? She was dying. There was no staying, was there?

"I can help you," he murmured. She could hear the smile in his voice. "Choose."

Lauren sighed again. Life was pain, and what did she have waiting for her? She felt lighter, and her grip on the real world loosened. Then something snapped, and she felt a jolt. She felt an instinct, clear and exact: she wanted to live.

There came warmth, washing over her soft and safe. Fear gripped her as she felt her senses return.

She screamed at the pain wrenching her body and felt as though she was being pulled apart. Her cries wracked her body; her throat was so raw she growled more than screamed. Every inch of her body was on fire, and she wanted to shut down again – retreat into safe, unfeeling darkness, where her own screams could not hurt her ears.

Another wave of tender heat hit her and took her pain away a little. Lauren panted between cries as the flood of agony eased, and she felt tears stream down her cheeks. She was aware of a hand holding hers tightly. It was a lifeline to her, and she gripped it, holding on as tightly as she could. An arm encircled her shoulders, and the tenderness emanating from this person covered her like a blanket.

"Breathe," he said.

Lauren obeyed, taking deep breaths the way she had been taught to do by her dad. The pain eased, and she opened her eyes. She blinked as the harsh light stung her eyes, making them water.

"Mother, blanket," the man said.

Lauren heard movement and felt herself being covered. She blinked again and looked to her right. A small gasp escaped her as she saw the face of the man who had spoken to her and still held her hand. The face was even more beautiful than the voice, if such a thing were possible. His skin was smooth; his lips were full. He had short, dark brown hair, and his eyes were an unusual violet colour. She was captivated by them and the way they shone. It was more than a twinkle; those eyes seemed to glow.

He was drenched with sweat, and as Lauren became more aware, she realised she was soaking too and completely naked under the blanket that had been thrown over her. The man was naked to the waist, and as she took in his carved physique, she observed that the jeans he wore had been put on in haste.

She frowned, wondering what had happened. The man smiled at her.

"Welcome back, Constable," he said.

He moved to let go of her hand, but she gripped it tightly, frightened that if he did let go, she would be lost.

She pulled her eyes from his and looked around. They were in her living room, or rather what was left of it. The sofa had been shredded and the furniture smashed or overturned. It reminded her of the countless burglary scenes she had attended.

Jack stood nearby; his face was pinched and pale, and if she had not known him better, she would have sworn he had been crying. Next to him was a woman that she felt she recognised, an older woman with close-cropped, bright pink hair and a wonderful woodland smell that seemed to welcome her home. Behind them stood officers in uniform; some were TSG, some were SO19, and some she knew from other teams. All of them shared a look of horror mixed with relief.

It overwhelmed her, all those eyes staring at her, and she wanted to back into a corner and hide.

"Please," she croaked. "I don't know who you are, but please don't let me go."

"My name is Marcus, officer. And I will not let go, if that is what you wish."

Again she quivered at his voice; damn, it was good.

Marcus looked up at Victoria. "Mother, please go and gather some suitable clothing for Officer Wylie." He then looked at Jack. "We need to take her to my private medical centre. They are the only ones able to deal with her condition."

Marcus shifted and looked back at Lauren. He smiled reassuringly at her. "We have to take you to a hospital, officer. I have to carry you out."

"Lauren," she said. "Call me Lauren."

She released his hand, and Marcus wrapped the blanket more securely around her. He then scooped her up into his arms as though she weighed nothing at all. Lauren winced as pain shot through her body, and she felt as though she had done the hardest workout ever.

As Marcus carried her out, Jack stepped forward and walked by her side.

"Lauren, I'll sort out your house and meet your parents at the airport." He took her hand and squeezed it.

Lauren looked past him and saw all the blood and carnage around her. Grief slammed into her heart, and her nose felt hot with tears as she realised her nightmare really had happened, that it had all been real. A chill shook her body, and Marcus seemed to hold her a little more tightly; his touch reassured her.

Victoria had grabbed a sports bag from one of the bedroom cupboards and filled it with clothing and toiletries, picking out Lauren's favourites by smell. She then looked for Lauren's bag which contained her phone, its charger, and a small purse.

Jack stood by the front door and had been talking on his mobile, arranging boarding up for the windows. Victoria tapped his arm. He looked at her, and the worry for his friend was etched on his face. She handed him a business card.

"Call this number, Sergeant. Moonscape will repair all of this damage," she told him. She pointed to a scribbled number. "This is my personal number. The others will stay and help you. They will do what you tell them to."

"Thank you, Ms Harper. Thank you for saving her," Jack said.

Victoria smiled. "Thank you for making me realise that not all police officers are the same," she responded. "And I think it is time you called me Vicky."

Jack smiled.

"When Lauren's parents arrive, call this number, and we will arrange for Stefan to bring you to the medical centre."

Jack looked towards the ambulance.

"She will be fine, now, Sergeant. Better than fine actually. You'll see when she settles."

Jack was not so sure. After what Lauren had become and the realisation of what she had done, how could she be fine?

"Will it always hurt her so much? The changing, I mean?"

"For the first few months, it will be agony," Vicky said. "The more she changes now, the more quickly it will hurt less, but it's natural to run from pain and avoid it, so she will have to get over that bit. Don't worry; we will help her through this."

Jack nodded, and Victoria left the house and walked over to the ambulance. Lauren had now been placed on a trolley bed and had a few more blankets covering her. The paramedics were contacting their control room, telling them where they would be transporting their patient.

The police officers stood around, staring at their colleague on the bed. She was one of their own and had very nearly died twice. Every single person in a uniform wanted to be in that ambulance and to not leave her side. The anxiety was powerful.

Marcus sat next to Lauren and took her hand again. Lauren had fallen asleep out of sheer exhaustion.

Victoria studied her son. For years she had been nagging him to find candidates suitable to be made his alpha. This poor police officer had been bitten against her will by a rogue, but Victoria could feel the alpha in her. She was incredibly strong for it to come through in the first Change and to have killed the wolf who had Bitten her, but who knew what affect being turned against her will and without preparation would have on her.

Victoria stepped into the ambulance and placed the bag on the seat next to Marcus and squeezed his shoulder. He looked up at her and gave her a strange, lopsided grin and then looked back at Lauren and gently picked a strand of hair from her brow.

Victoria could see he was smitten with her, and as she stepped out of the ambulance, she knew he was headed for disappointment. He did not know her and had not even Bitten her, and she had just come through a physical and psychological trauma – not the best situation to meet anyone in.

She stepped out of the ambulance, and the doors were slammed shut. As it pulled away, Victoria sighed. Now began the clearing up.

One month later

"The Independent Police Complaints Commission and the Metropolitan Police Press Office have today released the full disturbing footage from a custody suite from a police station in West London. This CCTV footage was recorded four weeks ago at the same time the reported werewolf killings took place in the same borough. Some of the film has already been publicised, as the wave of horrific killings also claimed the life of Inspector Katherine Kent and seriously injured another officer. The suspect was later named as Matthew Westmore, and he and his gang were killed in a police-related shooting a day later after attempting to kill several police officers and members of the public. The footage shows the suspect escaping from custody, and viewers should be warned that the images are extremely disturbing."

Jack looked up at the massive widescreen television fixed on the wall of the coffee shop. The video played again, the officers' faces pixelated out, for what had to have been the hundredth time since it had been released to the networks that morning.

The world had changed. As a police officer, Jack was used to being suspicious of everything around him and was more than used to the darkest, vilest things that humans could dole out to each other, but this was different. Now there were things in the world that he never had known existed, that chilled him to the bone.

He leaned back in the leather armchair and took a drink of his coffee. "So your boyfriend is putting up the money for the new unit and training programmes for TSG to combat supernatural creatures."

"He's not my boyfriend, Jack," Lauren said.

"Your alpha, then."

She shrugged. "He's not that either."

"Well, whatever he is, he wants me and the DI to be in charge of the new unit."

"What's it called?" Lauren asked.

"The Special Paranormal Investigation Team," Jack replied.

Lauren snorted with laughter. "Oh my God! Who came up with that?"

"You know the Met – some tosser wanting a promotion. Why don't you come and work for us? We could use a werewolf that's on our side."

She shook her head. "No, Jack. I'm going back to team next week. I'm a uniform, not a suit," she said. "Besides, shift work is better for me."

"You're going back to team?" Jack asked incredulously.

"Of course I am, Jack. I love team. Of course, the Met being the Met, they have had to dedicate a whole training day to educate them about my condition."

It was Jack's turn to laugh. "Really?" Who gave the training?"

"Vicky Harper."

Jack laughed louder.

"She ended up giving a dog-training session, as most of the team asked advice about how to handle their dogs. She then had to boil advice about me down to something like, 'If she's hungry, she needs a lot of food, and someone has to carry a bag for her and pick up her clothes when she Changes.' That was it, essentially."

"A whole training day for that? Well, there have been worse."

"It was at the mansion, and lunch was put on for us. We even got a tour of the facility, and my team got to see me Change, just so they could learn the initial signs and wouldn't get freaked out by it."

"Ouch," Jack said.

Lauren shrugged. "It still hurts, but not as much as it used to, and at I can control it now, which is good." She sighed. "I will be glad to get back to team and some kind of normality in my life."

"Well, we will keep a spot open for you on the team if you change your mind."

"Maybe for overtime, as you have a big shiny new budget funded by Moonscape," Lauren said.

"Funny, that's what most of you money-grabbing uniforms have said," he said and then looked at her evenly. "Tell me the truth, Lauren. How are you really?"

She met his grey eyes. "Truth? This is the most incredibly awesome thing to have happened to me," she replied with a grin.

He ran. The moment he spotted the two police officers on the High Street in their high-visibility jackets, he knew he had been rumbled. His photograph had been put in very shop window and every store manager of the shopping centre had been alerted that police were looking for him.

He had tried to disguise himself, but it had not been good enough. The security guard in the shopping centre had obviously recognised him and had contacted police via the radio link they shared.

So he ran down the alley which ran in between the fast-food restaurant and the coffee shop towards the car park and the new twenty-four-hour supermarket behind the High Street. He could lose the officers in the network of streets and alleys which lay between the town centre and the dual carriageway.

The officers gave chase; one gave commentary on the radio so the control room could direct other units to their location. This is what being a response team officer was about – not the paperwork but the catching of a criminal.

One of the officers tore ahead of her colleague, her stride strong and insanely fast. She bounded ahead, and as they ran across the crowded car park, he tried to elude her by changing direction. The officer followed, and her colleague moved to cut him off.

The suspect stopped in front of the male officer and went to punch him. Then he was flying through the air as the female officer slammed into him with the force of a truck. He landed on the pavement and was then aware of a clawed hand encircling his throat. There was no actual physical pressure behind that hand, but as her blue eyes glowed and stared down into his, he could feel the sheer weight of her superiority and knew she was an alpha.

Lauren grinned. "Hello, Daniel. I'm arresting you for suspicion of murder. You do not have to say anything, but …"

ABOUT THE AUTHOR

Susan Rae Glass studied performing arts at East Berkshire College at Langley, where she achieved a distinction in writing and devising and acting. She has written on and off since her teens in between several jobs the most recent being thirteen years in the civil service. She lives in Swindon, Wiltshire, with her white German Shepherd, who looks like a wolf, and her overactive imagination.

Lightning Source UK Ltd.
Milton Keynes UK
UKOW040608030513

210116UK00002B/58/P